i

LAST PAYS FOR ALL

A Tricky Dick Key West Mystery

by Jack Terry

The pride left his face. "*Every day, a little bit more goes away. You can drive fifty miles an hour, and soon it will start to feel too slow. You go sixty, and the same thing happens, so it becomes seventy, eighty, ninety. You keep pushing, because you have to, and before you know it, you don't recognize the person you were, perfectly content to be driving fifty miles an hour.*"

"*Why?*"

"*Why does the scorpion sting the frog? Because it's in their nature. Remember that Tricky, in everything you do. You can cut your hair, change your name, live in a new town, forge a different passport, but none of that will ever keep the frog safe when you're around.*"

The Tricky Dick Key West Mysteries

Talk Murder To Me
Traitor Vic's Rum Punch
Make Mine A Double
Red Skies At Midnight
Knee Deep And Rising

Other novels by Jack Terry

Chasing Ghosts

Last Pays For All

by

Jack Terry

Last Pays For All

Prologue

If you're in a book store, and you've picked this book up, and you're thinking that it sounds like a great book, there are two things you need to know:

1) It is.

2) This isn't where you start.

I mean, you can try if you want, but most of it won't make a bit of sense. That's because there are five books that come before this, books that have to be read in order, before you get to this one. You may think you're brave, that you can pick this one up and you'll have no problem figuring out what's going on. Now, I don't want to sound like I'm insulting your intelligence but let me tell you this:

The first thing that happens in the first paragraph of the first book is that a dead body is discovered, and the killer isn't revealed until about two/thirds of the way through this book.

I know, I know. Maybe I'm one of those guys who can't tell you how to get to the grocery store without rambling off into a dozen side tangents and taking forever. Or maybe, just maybe, you really should read the other five books first. You'll thank me later.

And, oh yeah. There may (or may not) be a talking manatee…

Terry

Last Pays For All

Chapter 1

"How did you know it would be me?"

"There are very few people who want to talk to me right now." The reality was, I thought there were several people who did want to talk to me, but they would prefer to do it in person. Makes it easier to shoot me. "Where are you?"

"You always know the best questions to ask." Her words were as easy coming and flirty as ever, but her voice wasn't as calm as she was trying to make it sound. "Too bad I don't have an answer that is as good."

"Any chance I can talk to whoever's keeping you company?"

"Let's find out." There was silence for a second, but nobody else got on the phone. "Hello?" Her voice was quiet, the sound of an indirect noise being filtered through a low-quality phone. I could tell from that it would do me no good to call out to her and tell her not to bother. She'd figure out soon enough that they had already left. Realizing that made her genuinely scared.

"I don't know where they are."

"Nowhere near you is the best I could come up with. That's a good thing, though."

"How is any of this a good thing, Tricky?"

"I was speaking relatively. If you have a free hand to use a phone, that means you have a free hand to work at freeing yourself. Start by taking off your blindfold."

"That's just it. I'm not wearing one. The room is just that

dark."

"There's nothing you can see? Not even a speck of light from where they taped over windows?"

"Nothing."

Lack of basements on this island notwithstanding, there were lots of places out there she could be, but not many of them would be perfectly sealed. Humidity has a way of warping wood, making even the flushest fitting door in the world eventually twisted just enough to let in some sliver of light. If that wasn't happening, it made me worried about being able to find her. I wasn't just keeping her on the phone simply because I liked the sound of her voice.

"Do me a favor. Yell out as loud as you can, but real short."

"Short?"

"Yeah. Just yell out the word 'Hey'."

"Ummm, okay." She did, and I realized I hadn't been specific enough.

"That was good, but I want you to do it again. And this time, hold the phone out at arm's length."

The phone sounded as shitty and cheap as I had expected, and the volume of her yell almost overloaded the technology, if you could call it that. But it wouldn't matter if she had the highest end phone on the market, or was calling me from the far end of a tin can and waxed string. In the flash of the moment after she stopped, the echo was distinct enough for me to hear.

The walls were metal. She was somewhere stuck inside a walk-in cooler. Which would explain why there was no light.

Of course, they also don't let in any air.

Last Pays For All

Chapter 2

I was torn between keeping her on the phone much longer or hanging up and blindly going out to look for her. The primary reason for staying on the phone would be to give us time to track the call. The problems with that scenario included the thickness of the walls distorting and blocking the signal. I started to rethink my low opinion of the phone. It must be something pretty powerful if it managed to make a connection through the walls – plus the fact that I'm sure the person or persons tracking the phone call weren't in much of a mood to help me.

I knew the Chief was tracking it, simply because I knew he was monitoring everything I did, from sneezing to screwing and everything in between. It was not a logical stretch to put a bug on the phone at the bar I was most likely to be at. However, the last interaction I had with the Chief was less than pleasant for all of us. At that time, he might have only been assuming, or maybe even poorly joking, about me killing Maples, but by now he had to know for sure. Regardless of how unofficial his official position was here, me taking out one of his players was not going to make him want to cooperate with me very much.

The reason I didn't want her to talk any more than she needed to was the obvious use of oxygen. If she was panicking, and I had to assume she was to a certain extent, she was already going to be breathing at a higher rate than normal. If I still forced myself to believe that she was a fashion writer/blogger/editor, then I had to believe that she had never been in this situation before, and it would be overwhelming to her. Recent events have made it clear she has other talents besides telling people how low to hang their hems, and some of those talents most likely led to having been in situations similar to this one. Practice may not make perfect, but it certainly makes one better at rolling with the punches. And that became the best reason I had for keeping her on the phone.

Naturally, I wasn't going to tell her that.

"Why did you have me do that?"

"It helped me figure out how big the room is. Knowing that lets me think of ways to help you escape."

"Escape?" She laughed, nervously bordering on hysterically. "I can't escape if I can't get out of the chair."

"I know, and that's the next thing we're going to work on. I'm guessing the free hand you have the phone in is the only limb free."

"Yes."

"Okay. Put the phone down in your lap, but carefully so it doesn't slip out. Then check your other wrist to see how it's fastened."

"Okay." There was silence for a moment, and then she was back. "Zip tie, pulled as tight as possible, and the excess cut off."

That was what I expected. "Check your feet for the same thing." I didn't think it would be any different, but I just wanted to give her something to do while I ran options through my mind. Before she could do that for me, she found something else to do.

"I'm an idiot. Hold on a second."

"What?"

Last Pays For All

"Just hold on." She continued to talk, but her voice was away from the mouthpiece again. Turns out, she was narrating for me what she was doing and why she was an idiot. "It's a phone. Phones have flashlights. I just need to figure out what kind of phone it is and how to turn it on."

If it was going to make her feel good, then I was going to let her do it, but it was obvious that when it came to phones, we were from the opposite sides of the tracks. She expected her phone to be a mini computer, with some advanced processing system, multiple forms of communication available, and certain basics embedded in the phone: a calculator, a map and, yes, a flashlight. My world was the world of burner phones, cheap disposable models that barely allowed you to send a text message, and even stopped lighting up the screen two seconds after the call was connected. In other words, phones without a flashlight. There was some hope that this phone was more like what she expected. Most burner phones drop service if they encounter a piece of tin foil, much less metal walls. But if this phone had a flashlight, the exasperation I heard when she spoke again told me everything I needed to know.

"I can't figure it out! How fucking hard can it be to turn on a flashlight?"

"Plenty hard if there isn't one there."

"Now isn't the time to be your typical asshole self," she reminded me, and I reminded her that I wasn't.

"It doesn't matter if there was one or not. Ain't nothing there in the light that isn't there in the dark."

"There could be, and it could help me get free."

"Yeah? And how would you get to it? Have you tried standing up yet?" Damn, I was being an asshole. Some things just come naturally, I guess. "I'm sorry. Forget it."

She didn't, because I could hear her struggle. "It isn't just that I'm stuck to the chair," she finally said. "The chair is somehow stuck to the floor. Hold on a sec."

I the phone being placed down, followed by the coming and going of her breath. When she spoke again, her voice was a little more lost.

"It's welded to the floor. They aren't fucking around."

'No, they're not,' I thought to myself, although who the chair had originally been meant for was still debatable. I had a feeling that she was a little small for it, but it would have fit me just fine. She then realized what I had figured out before. "Metal floor and no ambient light. I'm in a walk-in cooler, aren't I?"

"From the sound of it, probably, but look on the bright side." She went to correct me, but I cut her off. "I know, I know. Nothing about this qualifies as a bright side or a good side, but let me ask you this: are you cold?"

She had to think about it, simply because until she had figured out where she was, it wasn't something that struck her as being important. "Not really. Not as cold as I should be."

"Exactly. Which is why I know there's nothing there to help you escape."

"What?"

"I said that's why I know there's nothing there to help you escape. It's not turned on."

"You're breaking up on me." To confirm this, her voice had a touch of static to it when she spoke. Since I knew she hadn't moved, and neither had I, it meant the batteries were dying. I just didn't know if it was my phone or hers. Either way, I didn't have much time.

"Never mind that." I spoke slower and louder, as if a

dying phone was interchangeable with a foreign visitor. "Did they take Smitty with you?"

"What?"

"Smitty," I yelled. "Was he with you?"

"I haven't seen Smitty since the bar." Didn't quite answer the question, but under the circumstances, it was the best she could do. "Why...matter where...is?"

Last chance. "It might or might not," I told her.

"Wh..?"

"Your phone is dying! Can you hear me?" I stood up and started down the stairs, moving as fast as my busted-up knee would let me. Maybe if it was mine, it would be stronger closer to the base.

"...king up. I thi...one is dy..."

"Maybe it's mine. It's a cordless." I was next to the bar now. "Any better?"

"...don't leave me...how long...make it."

"I won't. I'll come find you." Then, not knowing what else to say, "Just sit tight." She managed to get one clear sentence out before her phone died for good.

"Like I have a fucking choice."

Terry

Chapter 3

There were a few people at the bar, but Ashley knew that whatever was going on with me was far more interesting than the same faces she saw every morning.

"Everything okay?" She knew it was a silly question the moment she asked it, but that didn't stop her.

"Peachy. You have your phone with you?"

"Yeah."

"What's your number?"

"305-555-1776."

I punched it in. From across the bar, we both heard the ringing a moment later. Instinctively, she moved to answer it.

"Don't bother," I told her as I hung up the phone in my hand. "Just had to confirm something."

I went behind the bar to put the phone back in the base, even though I knew it was charged enough already to not have been the one that had ended my conversation with Rachel. Standing next to the cooler, I went to help myself to a beer, but some sensible part of me told me that wasn't going to cut it. I had a long day in front of me, and there wasn't going to be any time to get a nap before it started. The coffee here wasn't great, but like I've told you before, it was convenient, and that was what mattered most.

I took the cup of coffee in one hand and Ashley in the other. "I need your help with something," I started to explain to her, but she had to explain something to me first.

Last Pays For All

"You might want to clean yourself up." She handed me a towel, and I saw that the movement had caused my knee to start bleeding again. Whatever had killed the poison had also done a number on the pain, and my hasty trip down the stairs, even though I hadn't felt it much, had torn open the freshly scabbed wound.

"Thanks. That could be awkward." I led her to the small strip of road shoulder that served as a scooter parking lot before leaning against a wall and pressing the towel on the wound. It was a safe guess that none of these scooters belonged to the members of the breakfast club. If those people rode anything at all, it was pedal powered. That meant they'd been left here the night before, and anyone who thought they were too drunk to drive a scooter would probably be too hungover to get up too early in the morning to retrieve it. "Besides the rentals, any of those scooters you don't recognize?"

"That black one, on the right."

"Any others?" The one she had picked out had custom work on it, meaning that anybody who recognized it would also probably recognize that I wasn't the owner, and I was trying to attract as little extra attention as possible.

"Either of those red and white ones." She pointed to two generic scooters. Those were a dime a dozen. If I was lucky, the two owners would come back at the same time and argue over who owned the one that was left behind. The other was going with me. I had questions that needed to be answered, and I knew where to go ask them.

"Perfect." The bleeding had stopped, and I tried to hand the towel back to her, but she thought better.

"Keep that. You might still need it, and I'm not sure there's enough bleach in the world to wash out those stains."

Terry

"Believe me," I told her as I moved, more gingerly this time, toward the scooter, "there never is."

Last Pays For All

Chapter 4

Saying I knew where to go get my questions answered might be a bit of a stretch, but for the time of day that it was, the C-Note would be my best option.

A lot of people who come down to Key West talk proudly about how they stayed out to last call. Drinking to four a.m. can be impressive, but what's really impressive, or pathetic, depending on how you look at things, is if you can then start again at seven a.m. when bars can reopen. Of course, just because you can, doesn't mean you do. A couple open at seven-thirty, and several more open at eight, but those places tend to be breakfast joints. People – tourists – don't look down at having a drink first thing in the morning if they can have eggs while they do it. Most of the places that are just bars, however, don't start raising their shutters until ten or eleven. Not the C-Note.

Seven days a week, they are open twenty-one hours a day. They seem to take just long enough to kick out the stragglers, lock the doors, count the money, stock the coolers, hose the place down, and start it all over again. And before you go casting judgement, keep one thing in mind: Some of the people down here don't get done working until five or six in the morning. (Somebody had to serve you while you insisted on making it until last call.) These people have every right, just like you and I, to want to relax and unwind with a drink or two after work. Some stop at Denny's, some will hang out with a friend (and fellow night

13

owl) at their place, some might even go home, take a shower and clean up because there just might be someone there they want to impress. Seriously. However it works, odds are good that if you get to the C-Note first thing in the morning, you'll see several of the people you tipped the night before. (Full disclosure. You will always undoubtably see people who were there until four the night before and went...well, somewhere for three hours. Wherever those three hours were spent, they did not include sleep or shower, but probably had some pharmaceutical enhancements. Believe me, these are not the people you want to talk to when you need some specific answers. On the other hand, if you have questions about the universe, they just might be the ones for you.)

I parked the scooter and headed indoors. They have an outdoor bar as well, but morning people at a bar aren't quite the same as morning people doing yoga on the beach. They like a little darkness with their eye-openers (or closers, depending where they were on their circadian rhythms.) As expected, there were a dozen or so people inside. I recognized most of them as being the same ones who were here when Rachel and I were incongruously drinking our champagne, which meant they weren't the people that could help me out. I ordered a beer and sat in the large window that faced the side street.

In the last six weeks or so, I'd been here twice. Being a person without island transportation and not usually in the mood to walk farther than I have to when it comes to getting a drink, this was something impressive. The problem with being back here, and not seeing the people I needed to talk to, was that it gave me time to think about those last two visits and the women that created them.

Last Pays For All

I failed Jessie, and the worst part was that I'll never be able to learn why or how I managed to do that. All the shrinks in the world could tell me that it wasn't my fault, that she got pushed down a dangerous path years before I became an even semi-present presence in her life because of her dad, but I was the last one left for her. I was the connection, and maybe instead of being a bridge to bring her out of that life and into a better one, I was her own personal Charon, slowly ferrying her down to an individualized hell she could never escape. Maybe it would have been better if I had walked away all those years ago and offered her a clean break from it all after her father died. I couldn't then; I promised her dad, and I felt like I owed her some reassurance that not everything in this world was bad, even if that was what I believed. I told myself back then I felt that she needed me in her life, just so she could have some image of stability, but who's to say I wasn't the one that needed her, just to have some connection to her father and his presence in my life? Thanks to a misguided trip to Cuba, I'll never be able to find out, or even to apologize to her for what happened. I failed Jessie, and now I was failing Rachel.

I was smart enough not to delude myself into thinking that Rachel's involvement had been my responsibility. What seemed to start off as an awkward introduction during an odd encounter, before turning into something approaching relationship normalcy, had finally been exposed along the way as a carefully choreographed event on her part. Finally knowing what the stakes were that everyone was playing for might have been the one piece of evidence I needed to fully understand it was business, nothing personal between us, no matter what she might have said, how she might have acted, or how I had responded. She played me for a fool, and even though I knew that was what was driving me now - the desire to clear my name, show that I hadn't been taken - I couldn't keep it in my mind. For some dumb reason, I cared about her. I couldn't understand and was doing my best to drown that feeling, even if it took the rest of my life. Knowing she was close to dying on my watch wasn't sitting well with me.

"Hey sailor. Buy me a drink?" The sweet voice took me out of my melancholy and I turned to see Scarlett standing at my elbow.

"I didn't imagine you to be a morning person."

"I'm usually not, but I may have made a mistake tonight." I could tell she wanted to talk about it, at least enough to pretend she was at confession, so all it took for her to open up was for me to cock my eyebrow. "It was a super slow night, and I knew I was going to be stuck there until the end, so when one of the girls offered, I figured what the hell, you know? I never do, you know that. Well, not never, but never enough that I might as well say never, but tonight, there was just something in the air, and I hoped it would get me through the last couple of hours, and then I could go home and if any edge was left, I knew there was a joint in the ashtray."

"Only..."

"Only I don't know where she got this stuff, or what she cut it with, but holy damn! I'm wired, and there ain't enough pot in the world to help me sleep now."

"I think the problem is that she didn't cut it with anything."

"If not, she better in the future! Too much of this stuff will kill a person." She thought about the absurdity of her statement. "Well, too much of anything will kill a person, I

16

guess. Anyway, about that drink." She winked and I capitulated.

"Okay, but it's going to cost you."

"Tricky, every free drink a woman gets costs her something in the end. They just don't always know it until it's too late sometimes."

Terry

Chapter 5

Some things never change. If you're pretty and you're popular, you can do things other people can't. I knew better than to try to ask, but when I mentioned that it'd be nice to talk somewhere quieter and with a little more privacy, she convinced the bartender to let us take our drinks to the outdoor bar. I took down a couple of stools on the far side, so as to not be seen by anybody else.

"So, what's on your mind?" She had taken the straw from her drink and was quickly rolling it up into a spiral before unrolling it, and then starting the procedure all over again.

"You know a lot of people, you know what's going on in town. I need some advice and information, and you're probably as good as anyone to help me."

"You mean as good as anyone you're going to find here and now."

"You got me."

"What's up?"

"I'm curious if you know of any vacant restaurants or bars that might be on the market."

"Doesn't matter if it's vacant or not. For the right price, every bar and restaurant is on the market."

"Maybe, but I'm looking for someplace that's currently not open."

"Why?"

"I'm thinking about going into business, opening my own place."

Last Pays For All

"You?" The look on her face said everything her words didn't. She knew I was about as serious as opening my own bar as she would ever be about joining the nunnery. But that's one of the good things about living in Key West. People here will readily believe any lie you tell them, especially if it's a harmless one, because they want to know that you'll be willing to believe theirs.

"Me. And I'd rather not have to deal with pre-existing conditions."

"You mean, like staff, management, stock and supplies, a customer base, things like that."

"Exactly. Less headaches that way."

"Makes sense, I guess." Okay, so maybe she wasn't completely buying my lie, but she was at least rolling with it. The good thing about pure cocaine – if good is a word that is at all applicable – is that it isn't cocaine that makes people paranoid but all the shit they cut it with to increase their profit margins. Anything of a lesser quality might have her asking me more questions, some that made sense and some that didn't, but instead she rolled through the inventory in her head.

"There's the old Brazilian steak place on Caroline that's been on the market for years, but that place is huge, and you don't want that. Other end of Caroline's is the old PT's, but that place has the kiss of death because it's too far away."

"Too far? Caroline Street's only like seven, eight blocks."

"Doesn't matter. Anything that's more than a block and a half from another bar is too far for tourists. And anything that's in Old Town isn't going to attract locals. What type of place are you looking for?"

"Not sure, but I'll know it when I see it." That was more of a truth than anything else I'd told her so far. She closed her eyes, her fingers still obsessing over the straw, while her mind ran through her rolodex. "Shit, I almost forgot. There are those two places on Duval, directly across from the Candy Striper."

"Where Pedro's Patio and The Turbo Charged Café are?"

"Were. You don't pay much attention, do you?"

"Those places never really catered to me."

"And well, not to anyone else either, I guess. The problem there is name recognition."

This honestly puzzled me. I don't know much, but I knew enough to know the first was part of a chain, a company with an outpost at every cruise ship stop, known for big drinks, cheap shots, and lousy "Mexican" food. And the second was based off a television show. I'm not sure what fixing junked hot rods had to do with selling burgers, but somebody had thought that could work. Apparently, they'd guessed wrong, but I brought it up with her anyway.

"Wrong kind of brand recognition. When people get down here, they've been given a list, the top ten things they're supposed to see when they're here, by friends who'd been here before, or, if they don't have friends, from some list they'd found online. If they're on a cruise ship, they barely have time to do half of what's on that list, so you know they're going to pass by anything that's not on it. And even if they're here for a few days, most people aren't adventurous enough to try new things. Besides, they are forty bars on that block alone, yet the landlords still think their property is worth something. Last I heard, one of them – can't remember which one – was on the market for twenty-eight thousand a month, plus triple net."

I wasn't sure what triple net meant, and I didn't really want to waste time finding out. "Any other places you know of?"

She went back to her mental rolodex, but now the cards were coming up empty. "Nothing I can think of. I'm sure there are places in midtown, there always are, but I try not to go past White Street if I can help it."

"Must make grocery shopping a bitch."

She flashed the same smile that I was sure was responsible for allowing us to come outside in the first place. "One of my regulars runs a delivery company. Food, booze, smokes, whatever you need for your vacation. He makes sure I never go hungry. Or thirsty."

"Or anything else."

"Nope. Strictly legal, no party favors. Besides, I told you, this was from a coworker." She finally realized how much overtime her fingers had been playing with her straw and dropped it like a hot rock. "I'm starting to feel like I might never calm down from this."

Her eyes let me know that she was seriously scared about that, and I figured the least I could do was offer to help.

"Tell you what. I need to get dressed better, and I might have something on the boat that'll help you calm down. Besides, it'll give you a little more time to think of other places."

"Oh Tricky, you're so charming. I wish I could say that was the first time I heard that pick-up line from someone trying to get me on their boat." Her reaction was such a natural one to shooting down over-eager clients in such a disarming manner that she even patted me on the face, and between that action and her tone of voice, she made me feel like my offer had been nothing but an ulterior motive all along.

"I didn't mean that at all. I was serious. I mean, you see

the outfit, not exactly real estate shopping clothes. And I do have something that'll bring you down." Several things, I'm sure. The trick would be remembering which one works best and where I left it.

"It's okay, Tricky," her mouth still smiling but her eyes still scared. "You didn't hear me say no."

I led her to my scooter. "Where'd you park?"

"Park? I know better. Captain Taxi was my chauffeur tonight." She climbed on the back. "And, um, are we going to talk about this?" She drew a circle in the air, encompassing me.

"I told you, I know I need to get back to the boat and get changed."

"You going to change your knee, too?" I said nothing as I started up the engine, and she continued. "Nobody's going to rent a bar to someone that's going to turn it into a shooting gallery."

Last Pays For All

Chapter 6

I slid the scooter back into its original parking spot. Nobody was there creating a commotion, and I felt like I had hidden the damage from hot wiring it well enough that nobody would ever be the wiser. I skipped us past the bar and got her in my dinghy. I figured I'd spent enough time there recently.

Back on my boat, I didn't have time to tell Scarlett to sit tight while I went below deck. "This is awesome," she called out, probably a bit more excited than she would normally be about a boat. "This is perfect."

"For what?" I popped open a porthole, as much to let some fresh air into the cabin as to be able to continue talking to her while she made her way to the bow. Her voice might carry, but mine was tapping into its reserves.

"For sunbathing naked. The fewer tan lines I have, the more money I make."

"My neighbors might not mind seeing you like that, but I'm not sure they'd appreciate me doing it." If I wanted to know, I guess I could have asked them. I'd given them plenty of opportunity to examine the goods over the last several weeks.

And there it was again.

Six weeks ago, I, being of a reasonably sound mind and body, had given Rachel a playful and somewhat innocent encore of the naked interpretive dance performance I'd presented to the world a few nights earlier. How was that even possible? Two months ago, I didn't know Rachel, I barely knew Scooter, and I had all but forgotten about the Chief. Certainly, I never expected him to infest my little corner of paradise. I had managed to put all of my old life so deep behind closed doors that I could live perfectly freely, no cares and no concerns. It wasn't even that I could start to become the person I always wanted to be, rather I simply just became that person overnight. But all it took was a dead body, a pair of black panties, and a devil from my past to blow that door off the hinges.

Suddenly, I felt very tired. Not just "Hey, I've been up all night in the strangest way possible" tired, but right down to my bones. Because now I finally knew that none of this would ever be behind me until all of it was. I could sail wherever, I could do whatever, I could change my name to whichever character I stumbled across in a book, all to leave the old me behind, but none of that would matter. It would always, always, be who I was. Even if I burned it all down and left the ashes behind, I'd still be taking the worst of it with me. There were only two options left, and since I could not possibly see how I would ever be at peace with my past, where I could maintain that balance, the last option was the best.

But not yet. Regardless of what I told the Chief, I was going to finish this through. That, and that alone, woke my bones up enough.

Without having a detailed inventory, I had to guess where I'd hidden all of my treasures. Hers was simple enough, the most time consuming being the tea I had to turn it into. On the aft deck, I started the water to boil before heading back down to take care of me. Stitches might come in handy, but I didn't have the time, so instead I ground up some flower petals from Bolivia that an old friend had passed on to me and rubbed them into the wound before applying fresh gauze and a bandage. When I was done, it looked like nothing more than the remnants of getting a fresh tattoo.

The poison was another question. Whatever antidote I had taken was miraculously good enough to keep me alive, but I didn't know if it was killing the poison or just holding it at bay. Luckily, my Bolivian friend had given me a few things, one of which was the ultimate cure-all. It came with an orchestra full of side effects, ones I'd be dealing with for the next twenty-four hours, but it was a price worth paying in the meantime.

I brought Scarlett her tea, and that was when I discovered that she hadn't been kidding about no tan lines and naked sunbathing. "Is it even possible to get a tan this early in the morning?" I asked her as I handed the mug to her.

She propped herself up on an elbow. "Down here, it's always possible. Number one complaint I hear about when giving a lap dance is how these weekend warriors from Wisconsin can't understand how they got so sun burned so quickly." She coughed up the first sip of tea. "God, that's awful."

"Most of them are, but you ain't drinking it for the flavor."

"Definitely not." She took another sip, grimacing only half as much as the last time. "How long before it starts to work?"

"Not very. You'll want to be thinking about calling your chauffeur within the next fifteen minutes."

"Good. That gives me more time to enjoy the sun." Even though there was still steam coming off the mug, she forced the rest of it down quickly before laying back on the deck. "This must be a great place to just relax and let things go."

"I can't complain."

"Mmmmmm, I bet. Good space to come out and clear your head, help yourself think through all your problems."

I looked over at her, willing myself to be distracted by her, wanting to find some way to make the next five or ten minutes pass by without me setting up shop in my head, but I couldn't even continue talking. Normally the shameless flirting and double entendres, the stock in trade for a bachelor like me, would be easily flowing, but not today. Instead I slid to the bowsprit, dangled my legs over the railing, and waited for something that wasn't going to happen.

Something was eating away inside my mind, but without someone specific – something specific – to talk to about it, it would never become clear.

And that had been clear this morning when he told me goodbye.

Last Pays For All

Chapter 7

Scarlett's taxi was waiting for her when we got there, and the cocktail I'd mixed up for her was starting to kick in, so I gave the driver an extra twenty to make sure she not just got home but got inside as well.

"No worries, Tricky," he assured me. "Many of her clients tend to be some of my best customers."

With her taken care of, I needed to do some more research. It wasn't that I didn't trust her short list of possible vacant restaurants and bars, it was that I knew it wasn't exhaustive enough. Ten minutes on the library computers confirmed as much for me. There had to be a dozen places, scattered all over the island, that looked like they'd have the type of walk-in cooler Rachel was slowly dying in. Even on my own with a commandeered scooter, it would take me most of the day and some of the night to check them all out, not to mention risking arrest with the B&E most of them would involve. That bothered me far more than the stolen scooter aspect of the plan, but only because it's easy to convince someone they'd forgotten where they parked their scooter, thanks to the seven Painkillers Zach and Andy had made for them the night before. Kind of harder to explain being on the wrong side of a locked door.

The second choice wasn't a choice at all. It would take two hours minimum just to get an appointment with a real estate agent, plus another thirty minutes to convince them that I needed to see all the locations on the list, then convince them that my mind would be made up about fifteen seconds after getting there, and finally culminating with having yet another innocent bystander being dragged into this mysterious maelstrom.

Choice three was no better, because it was no more logical. Not knowing who the person was that was behind everything, much less what their ultimate goal was for killing Scooter and all the ensuing shit that followed, meant I could sit here all day in the air conditioning, trying to get inside the mind of a criminal, and still end up with nothing more than an uneducated guess. Certain situations seemed to follow certain rules, rules that in this case had been disregarded even before the dominos had started falling. The only choice I had was choice four, and I knew two things about it: It could work, and it wouldn't work, because it would involve me having to suck up to the Chief. I'm not typically a man of contrition, but I knew I had to come up with something to say to the Chief if I wanted him to do anything for me. Best I could hope for was to lean on the fact that he and Rachel had formed some sort of a relationship over me and beyond me. They'd been working together for some reason, and hopefully whatever that reason was, it was good enough to make him give a shit. Of course, the way people were seemingly changing sides in this opera, he might be the one responsible for her kidnapping.

Before I got halfway to the station, I caught sight of something that made my blood run cold. Down the street, in front of my favorite breakfast spot, was a run of yellow police tape.

Maybe the walk-in cooler hadn't been abandoned at all.

Last Pays For All

Chapter 8

I'm not sure if this is something new with people, or my awareness of it has simply increased the older I've become, but when I got to the crime scene, the first thing I saw were people complaining that they couldn't finish their breakfast. They were genuinely up in arms about their breakfast being cancelled, which of course meant their vacation had been ruined, and if they weren't allowed to finish eating, they were certainly going to Yelp all about it and believe you me, we'll have this place shut down in a week. I felt bad for anyone who worked there, because every one of them was getting an earful of shit from someone. The guy I felt least bad for was the dishwasher, though, because I knew for a fact he spoke one hundred percent Haitian and zero percent English. At least he was smart enough not to smile at the insurance-salesman-looking middle-aged man who was listing all the places he could have gone instead, where he certainly would have had a better time.

The rookie at the police tape didn't recognize me, but Suarez, standing at the bar where there was more yellow tape surrounding a white sheet, did, and waved me in. The fact that the dead body wasn't in a cooler did nothing to lessen my apprehension. Smitty was still missing, and nothing sent more of a message than a public execution.

"Please tell me this doesn't come back to me."

"That's an odd opening statement to someone I wasn't even going to give a witness interview to. You got something else you want to tell me?"

"Hopefully not, but you tell me first. Who is it?"

He pulled back the sheet so I could see the face. "Recognize him?"

Of course I did. Most people would. But most people probably couldn't admit to having just seen him about three hours ago. I'd figured he would have been safe, hardly being part of my orbit at all. Looks like my orbit might be getting bigger, but I had to find out for sure. "What happened?"

"Three witnesses all say the same thing. He was talking with a couple of people, other locals, about politics, when someone sitting down by the coffee machine commented. Nobody remembers exactly what was said, only that it was pretty clear they had a large difference of opinion. The bartender tried calming things down, but then there was a news story about something – once again, nobody remembers what – and they both started at it again. Our vic, wanting to prove he was right, ends his last statement with a pretty sharp insult about the perp's parents. The perp, wanting to prove he was righter, pulls a piece and shoots him twice in the face."

"Welcome to the era of civility. You got the perp?"

"Yeah, he really had nowhere to go. Some guy sitting down heard the gunshots, jumped the little fence and pinned him down."

"Where is he now?"

"Inside. Why, you afraid you might know him too?"

"Something like that, yeah."

The a/c was running inside, and my sweat went clammy. It may be hard to understand where the line was of people I knew who were targets versus the people that weren't, but in my mind, it made sense. More importantly, it was a hard and fast line, and if these...people, groups, nations, whoever was fucking with me, didn't see it that way, but rather as a purge against anyone who's even ever heard my name, then there was no telling how this would all end. I did a quick inventory of what I could say that would convince anyone who wasn't him or I to leave the room so we could talk, but I took one look at the guy and felt relieved.

When you hire a hit man, you're looking for someone who can blend in with a crowd. Believe it or not, they aren't all well-dressed eastern European guys with sharp cheek bones or ex-Green Berets who look just a bit too much like the Brawny paper towel man. Most hitmen look something like the guy delivering your mail, or the gal collecting the offerings in your church. That being said, no matter how much they don't look alike, if you've seen enough of them in your life, both those shooting at you and those shooting for you, you see the common traits they have. This guy so clearly did not have them, I had to make sure I stepped quickly back into the heat before I started laughing.

I lit a cigarette as the EMTs were loading the body onto the stretcher. "He's about two months too early."

"Fine with me. One less yokel the FWC will have to worry about during mini-season."

"I hope he enjoyed his last one. Gonna be many seasons from now before he sees the sunshine side of a prison."

"You serious? In this state, he'll find the right lawyer who will petition for the right judge with the right jury. He gets one jackass on that jury who wears the same robes as this guy, and the only guilty verdict returned will be concealed weapon or illegal discharging. He'll get credit for time served and be back here chasing bugs and bragging about this killing by next summer."

Terry

I never realized Suarez could be so cynical. To me, he had always been just a little too simple and a little too slow to develop such feelings. "It sounds like you need a vacation. Someplace far away from people. Is the Chief coming down?"

"No. He's got some other paperwork he needs to deal with." He finally looked up from his notebook. "You don't really want to talk to him, do you?"

"What I want and what I need are two vastly different things. Thanks for letting me in. I'll see you."

I walked out behind the stretcher, and Suarez called to me as I crossed the dining patio. "Watch your step down there, or anywhere for that matter. Some people don't know what happened to Maples, but some people do. And even if he wasn't liked by most of them,"

"Or any of them," I corrected him.

"Or any of them, he still wore the blue. And that makes those people like him a lot more than they like you."

I felt like saying something about me being unofficially forced into the blues for the last six weeks, but I let it go. So much of what had been going on was on a need-to-know basis, and he didn't need to know any of it. "Thanks for the heads up, but I'll be careful."

I mean, I was already used to everybody else seemingly wanting to kill me. The cops were just some more names on an already overcrowded list.

Last Pays For All

Chapter 9

Suarez's warning was not unfounded and not incorrect. The sergeant at the desk obviously hadn't heard all the details, otherwise I'm not sure he would have let me in back as quickly as he did. But there were a couple of uniforms that walked by me, one making sure to give me as wide a berth as possible, and the other redirecting himself so his shoulder met mine. I saw it coming, and I could have done something about it, moving aside or leaning in, but now was not the time to make a stand one way or the other. I just kept my head up and my eyes focused straight ahead.

I closed the door behind me and sat opposite the Chief. As advertised, he was doing paperwork, and spoke without looking up.

"If it's anyone other than you, now's not the time for you to be here and you better leave." He gave me exactly five seconds to stay seated, proving that Daniel had come into the lion's den before he spoke again. "If it is you, you better pray to whatever God abandoned you to this lifestyle all those years ago, to strike you dead now before I do it myself."

"Those are pretty harsh words, especially coming from the person who brought me into this lifestyle. And believe me, you're about the farthest thing from a God."

He made no effort to speed up or stop what he was doing, and the time passed. It was a game of chicken, each of us seeing who was going to blink first, and he knew he had the upper hand. My patience could only last so long, and I had to hope it lasted longer than the oxygen inside wherever Rachel was holed up.

He took his time, I'd like to think more than he needed to, but he made it clear that everything and anything was going to be a bigger priority than me. When he was done, I was almost surprised he didn't purposely get up for a cup of coffee or something else, just to ice me. Instead he just looked over the desk, realized all the old business was done, and turned his attention to the new business at hand.

"Do you know how much you have fucked up my life?"

"Do you know how little I know you actually care?"

Harsh but true, and for the same reason Suarez tried to warn me about the reception I might get from the other cops. You may have someone you can't stand, someone who is the community punching bag, the one that everybody agrees on not liking, but when somebody from outside your community says anything, you'll be the first to stand up for their defense. The cops were that way about Maples, but the Chief was no cop, and if he had to pick sides in this battle, it was me he was going to stand behind.

I wasn't deluding myself into thinking that was because he actually cared. The closest it came to that was the bonding of shared experiences, and I'm not talking some corporate weekend retreat, trust fall and ropes course, let's all sit around the fire and pay each other three compliments before we sing "Kum Ba Ya" and make s'mores weak-ass shared experiences, but the shit he and I saw throughout the years. He may not like me much, but he respects me enough for me to know that, in the middle of everything, me being protected was more important than Maples being dead.

"Personal feelings for the deceased notwithstanding, this

one is a little harder to sweep under the rug than the rest of the bodies you've been piling up around here."

"I haven't killed that many people," I reminded him.

"Normal members of society don't typically have to defend their lifestyle by using the phrase 'killed that many people.' And it isn't just the ones you've killed, but also the ones that have been killed in your wake. You're bad news for life insurance adjusters."

"All things you knew when you foisted this case on me to begin with."

He leaned into the desk. "And I'll tell you again now what I tried to get through your head then. Is there anyone else that could have done it? Certainly nobody down here. The talented cops are too corrupt, and the earnest cops are too vulnerable. If this had been left up to the rank and file, Maples would be alive and the case would be closed, unsolved, and Suarez would be dead from not so natural causes, leaving behind a wife, family, and more questions than answers about what really happened."

"That still brings me back to my original question: why should I give a shit about any of this?"

"Because you do, whether you want to or not. You may just be the most warm-hearted, cold-blooded killer I've ever met."

"Thanks, but I don't think Hallmark makes a card expressing that emotion. But I ain't here to talk about Scooter. I'm here to talk about Rachel."

He kicked back in his chair, lacing his fingers together before resting the back of his head in them. "Sorry, but I can't help you find somebody who's already dead."

Terry

Chapter 10

I immediately understood what he meant about me being both warm-hearted and cold-blooded. Hearing him say she was dead unleashed an unexpected torrent of emotions through me: sadness for her loss, disbelief that it could be true, anger that I hadn't saved her in time, and betrayal that he would allow it to happen. That was the warm-hearted part of me, but my cold-blooded nature shut it all down, so when I spoke, it was measured, precise, and clear.

"You better not be telling me that you beat me to where she was this morning, and decided it was time to take care of another loose end."

He did a good job of looking thoroughly confused. "What are you talking about? She's been dead since yesterday."

It was my turn to look dumbfounded, and this I wasn't faking. "You talking about the stiff that we looked at in the beer cooler? I told you, that wasn't her."

"And as much as I would have liked to believe you, we both know you're no expert on postmortem investigations. Luckily, there just happened to be an expert at Boca Chica, so we brought the body to him for a positive ID."

There was no way this was logically possible, but the logic was swimming upstream against a heady current that I couldn't understand. I had a dozen reasons not to trust her, half as many questions concerning who she really was and what her endgame was, and the fact that I had spoken to her not three hours ago. I knew that hadn't been her in the beer cooler last night, but every time the Chief even intimated that Rachel was dead, it stung just like another tiny cut.

"Chief, I know who that woman was. I mean, I don't know exactly who she was, but I know about who she was in general to be able to tell you specifically who she wasn't. Rachel."

He reached into the stack of paperwork he'd been filling out when I came in and pulled out a sheet of paper. I'd seen enough of them in my life to know I was looking at a death certificate, and my eyes knew exactly where to go to find the name of the deceased.

Rachel Smith.

Terry

Chapter 11

I didn't want to believe that it was true, but I couldn't make myself not believe it. I looked through the entirety of it, trying to find some inconsistency, but everything was where it was supposed to be, saying what needed to be said. The details of the car accident, the report of the injuries, the comparison of the dental records, everything. There was no mention of the melted hunk of metal I'd pried out of her bones, and nothing of the accelerant that finished the job, but that was superfluous. At some point, the certificate might have to be released if a reporter came sniffing around for answers. If the accident had included such a spectacular fireball that several of the witnesses commented on, I'm sure it was the front page of today's paper - provided that some old lady hadn't yelled at the tree commission the night before, becoming the lead story – but any story that came out that quick, would be light on specifics and include the phrase "the identity is being withheld until the next of kin has been notified." Theoretically, the Chief could stonewall the reporters indefinitely, because even if he put all the resources at his fingertips into action, finding a next of kin was going to be impossible. But, there was one detail on the certificate that stood out to me, that told me he wasn't going to do that and would have no problem releasing this cleaned up version of the truth to whoever had a press badge and a pad, and I called him on it as I threw the report back across the desk.

Last Pays For All

"You probably should have at least come up with a less generic last name. One that actually came closer to her ethnicity."

"Which was?"

"Predominantly Northern European and Mediterranean, with a little Eastern European thrown in for flavor."

"She tell you this?"

"She didn't have to."

"Fine." He slid the paper back inside the stack. "Suppose I do that. Is it going to matter?"

It would, but not for any practical reasons. I knew by this point that Rachel was as much her real name as Richard was mine, but I felt it was important for some reason that, in death, she be remembered at least somewhat for who she really was and where she came from. Some way of honoring her past, her true past. Not only who she had become throughout her life, but where she had come from originally. I knew it was a sentimental thing to be feeling, but I couldn't let it go. It was like I needed closure.

Except for the one part of my brain that was working this morning, reminding me she wasn't really dead in the first place.

"This is a nice piece of paper, and you'll have to explain to me sometime why it exists, but it's a bit premature and awfully inaccurate. I talked to her this morning."

"You sure about that?" He got that look of befuddlement back on his face. "I'm pretty sure this is how she dies. She made sure we got all of the details correct."

Before I could say anything, ask anything, he started laughing. "I don't know what has gotten into you, Tricky, but you are certainly not as sharp as you once were."

"Blood loss, lack of sleep, poisoning, dead bodies,

unanswered questions." I spelled out the list for him. "But none of that explains what the fuck you're talking about."

"She asked me to do her a favor, declare her dead. So, I did."

"When did she ask you to do this?" I needed help establishing a timeline. By now it had been almost twenty-four hours since I'd seen Rachel. With that kind of lead time, she could honestly be anywhere in the world. I only assumed she was still in Key West because that's where all the fun was. But if she talked to the Chief after the body had been found, or even better, after I'd gone spelunking through it on top of a collection of beer cases, it made the window of movement much smaller. Yes, she still could have gotten smuggled to the airport, thrown on a private plane and flown to God knows where (knowing what I finally did about who was shaping up to be behind all of this, money was certainly not an impediment to getting things done), but that would be less likely. The Chief threw cold water all over my hopes.

"A few days ago. She came up to me and talked to me about it."

"What, exactly, did she say?"

"Told me she was tired of you, and the only way you'd leave her alone was if you thought she was dead." He cocked an eyebrow at me, loving the fact that he had me by the short hairs. "Too soon? No, she just felt like things were wrapping up, and when that happened, all the loose ends were going to be taken care of one way or another. I owed her a favor, so I obliged."

"She knows that some municipal paperwork from some city employee isn't going to mean shit to the people who might be looking for her."

"No, but having that body helps."

"Yes, but those same people probably know who that body really is. Probably are even the ones that made her dead."

He shrugged his shoulders. "I just did what she asked me to. How well it works out for her depends on how she lives her life after this is all done."

"And I'd like her to continue living her life. I know you were bugging the phone at Barnacle Bob's, which means I know you were tracing the call. Where is she?"

"I told you Tricky. I can't help you find somebody who is already dead."

I surprised myself with how quickly I was across the desk, and that meant I did a good job of surprising him as well. The chair collided with the wall, throwing both of us to the floor. He played the part of a cop perfectly, including the complete uniform. The problem that caused for me was to make sure he couldn't access any of the weapons he had on his belt while simultaneously getting a weapon of my own on him. There are things you can't plan for, and dumb luck in your favor is one of them. The chair rolled free as I rolled on top of him. Getting a foot on each of his wrists, I leaned back on his legs and pinned the chair under his neck firmly with one hand.

The other hand had my gun pointed at his forehead.

He laughed, as much as he could, as he struggled to breathe. "You might as well pull that trigger quickly, because the longer we wait here, the sooner someone's going to come through that door saying 'Chief, I heard a noise.' What are you going to do then?"

"I killed one cop today. I'll kill another. And then I'll kill you last."

Terry

"What if it's Suarez?"

I cocked the hammer and pressed the chair harder. "He better hope it's not."

He laughed again and waited. And waited. And waited some more. Finally, he understood what was happening.

None of the cops may have particularly liked Maples, but he was one of theirs and they would protect him. And they also knew that even though Chief wore the uniform, he wasn't one of theirs, and they could give two shits. They knew he was one of mine, and they were probably hoping we'd do them all a favor and just kill each other right now, an outcome that was probably dangerously close to happening.

"Best we could do is Old Town somewhere, six block radius, with the original city hall right in the middle," he told me. "The signal was weak, and her phone died before we could lock it."

"You better be telling me the truth."

"You better start moving fast."

Last Pays For All

Chapter 12

It turns out my trip to the library was probably unnecessary. Scarlett's list of closed restaurants and bars matched what had been listed online, and they were the only ones within that same six block radius the Chief had talked about. Hindsight being what it is, this knowledge just made me pissed off with myself, because now I felt like I'd wasted an hour. All I'd learned in that time was that Rachel was legally dead, and that didn't strike me as something worth knowing. I'd probably end up being wrong about that later, but right now I was just more concerned with her being mostly dead, and not legally so.

Three of the four places were within a block of each other, but they couldn't be more different from one another, specifically one from the other two. If you've never been here, what Scarlett was saying about a place being too far away when it's only a few blocks from Duval might sound strange, but you didn't even have to go that far to be far away. The first building was a half a block away, and that was enough to help make it invisible to people. Granted, the location had several other problems, the biggest being it was massive, and the owners incorrectly assumed the fad of Brazilian all-you-can-eat steak houses from several years back would be a boom and not a bust, but the block it was on was just quiet enough that the vast majority of people would walk right by it, stumbling from one big name place to another, without pulling their eyes up from the map.

Terry

As if to prove her point, when I got there, I saw that the bar next to it, one that had been three different names in the last three years, had its windows papered over and its signs taken down. Add it to the list of places I needed to break into.

A quiet side block was obviously a blessing, in order to help me accomplish the breaking and entering. I slipped down the service alley that ran behind both places, unconsciously whistling "King of the Road" while I was looking for a lock that wasn't locked because nobody was around. The old steak place was locked up tight, and the grit I found on the lock and handle gave the appearance there hadn't even been a showing of the place in several months, much less an offer. The new old bar next door, however, was far more casually closed up. It had the look of an expected return any minute, and since I didn't want to be here when that happened, I decided to get in and out as soon as possible.

The bar turned out to be a bust. They must have been partnered up with one of the major bars on Duval Street that they backed up to and shared their resources. In this case, that would mean shared cooler space because there were none, except for the standard six footers behind the bar. And I knew Rachel was flexible, but even in the dark, she would have been able to point out to me if she'd been in something that small.

I made my way through the room to the wall that the bar shared with the steakhouse. I almost felt like I could write it off as well, seeing as how dirty the door had seemed from the outside. That would give me time to move on to the next place that much quicker, but it would also kill me if I simply played my hunch and didn't give it a walk-through. Besides,

Last Pays For All

I don't know much about kidnapping, but I felt like it was a safe bet that the last thing you wanted to do was leave obvious clues of where your secret hangout was.

Clues like a freshly cleaned door.

I was coming up empty when I checked the wall. There was no ductwork that ran between the two buildings, nothing in either of the bathrooms that suggested a connection, not even a hatch to an attic crawl space that might give me another way in. I almost dismissed the closet that sat between the two bathrooms – it was a closet after all, what help could it be? – but I felt duty-bound and checked it out. I was so nonchalant and doubtful that I had to force myself to take a second look because my first passing glance barely registered at all. The second look was worth it.

The back wall was a mosaic of shoddy paint jobs, presumably done over the years as the place changed hands and names. I get the need to redecorate a place just so you can have your own personal stamp on it, but I didn't understand why that had to include the janitorial closet. Mops and brooms and shop-vacs work just as well, no matter what color the walls were. The thing was though, you'd think, with so many coats of paint, any imperfections in the wall would be eliminated, covered over. Which made it odd that I could see an almost perfectly straight line running from the floor almost to the ceiling, indented into the wall. And at the almost ceiling point, there was another almost straight line, also indented, that almost ran to the edge of the perpendicular wall.

Put all together, it almost looked like a door.

Terry

Chapter 13

They'd done a reckless job of cleaning behind the bar when they closed up shop, which was beneficial to me because I needed the knife I'd found. The paint was thick, the knife was dull, but within a few minutes I'd managed to work it in deeply enough to find out my hunch had been right. It was a door, buried under what looked to be a dozen or so layers of paint. Each layer seeped a little further into the gap between the door and the doorframe, but thankfully, persistent humidity and shoddy construction had allowed for a larger space than normal, which gave me more wiggle room to get the blade all the way through the layers. Once that was accomplished, it was just a matter of muscling the knife down to the floor.

Luck was on my side, which meant the hinges were on the other, opening the door into the steak house. A few shoulder blows finally separated the wood from the paint, and the door creaked open. It was both comforting and disappointing that my entrance hadn't been greeted by the sound of gunfire. Disappointing because it meant there probably wasn't anybody here, watching over a kidnap victim. Comforting because I'd already been shot once recently, and it was nice to not have gotten shot again. The bar had been dimly lit, the ambient light from the street diffused by the curtained windows and dusty air. But it had been high noon compared to what was greeting me now. Whoever the realtor was, they must have assumed that anyone trying to look in the large plate glass windows that made the front wall would be disappointed by what they saw, so they had covered them with blackout curtains. The only light I had was what had come with me from the bar, and I couldn't take it with me.

Luckily, every restaurant is designed pretty much the same and I fumbled my way back through what had been the kitchen. I knew to expect two walk-ins: a larger cooler and a smaller freezer. I moved as carefully as I could, trying hard not to make noise. The lack of gunfire didn't mean that there wasn't somebody there anyway, waiting to ambush me. It may sound conceited to say this, but I was starting to feel like I was more valuable to anybody and everybody involved in this shit show alive than I was dead, and random gunfire in the dark doesn't do much for keeping a person alive. But the only sound I heard in the silence was the occasional squeak of a rat moving around the fringes of the room. If there was somebody waiting for me, they were certainly earning their pay.

Soon enough, I found the familiar stainless-steel wall, letting me know where I was. Running my hand at waist height, I bumped into the handle. With no padlock to stop me and no reason to wait, I opened the door and stepped into an even darker (if that was at all possible) void.

"Rachel?" I know, it's only one word, but believe me, I barely got that word out before I almost threw up. Apparently, when the owners had packed up, they decided the equipment was far more valuable than the food, because they had taken all of the former and left behind all of the latter. I had never been more thankful for near perfect darkness, because I had no desire to see what was moldering in front of me. I had been to some nasty places and I had smelled some horrific things, but none of that matched up to the explosion of rank that greeted me.

I have to give credit where credit is due, though. The seal on that door was perfectly air tight. I hadn't been able to smell anything before I'd opened the door, and neither had the rats. But they did now. They must have known something was waiting for them ever since the place closed, and they had stayed in the neighborhood, in hopes of someday finding this bonanza, because I could hear what sounded like a dozen of them suddenly scurrying across the floor. Not wanting to feel the sensation of them crawling over my feet, not expecting that Rachel would be in the other walk-in, and not needing to experience that level of revulsion again upon finding a whole new world of rot, I made my way back to the relative brightness of the bar and on to the next location.

Last Pays For All

Chapter 14

The Mangrove Bar sat kitty-corner from Pedro's Patio and The Turbo Charged Café, close enough that I could keep an eye on them, but not so close that it looked like I was keeping an eye on them. It might seem like an extra level of paranoia, but it had a greater purpose than that. Yeddie was working, and he knew both buildings I was concerned about, having had worked there when he first got to the island. He wasn't buying my "I want to go into the bar business story" any more than Scarlett had been, and he was far more willing to call me out on it.

"I'll tell you what, Tricky. Instead of going through all the headache of doing that, I'll make it easy on you. You just give me fifty thousand dollars a month. And at the end of each month, what I haven't managed to spend, I'll light on fire and flush the ashes down the toilet. And we'll keep doing that until you decide you don't want to be in the world of bar ownership anymore."

"Why would I want to do that?"

"Because that's all you do when you own a bar." He rolled the toothpick from one corner of his mouth to the other. "And I'm making it easy on you. I'm not requiring you to put out any of the up-front capital it takes to sign the lease, plus whatever repairs and renovations would be necessary. And I'm also eliminating all the penalties and fees that come with breaking a lease early. Hell, I'm being downright generous."

"Let's say I'm too stupid to take your advice. What can you tell me about those places?"

He shook his head at me, letting me know I was stupid for thinking he believed me and he felt stupid for going along with it. "On the left, you got the open space in front, it runs to the right and opens up a bit more in the back, like a patio. Great place for live music, except for the guest house in the back and their stuffy clientele. One of the reasons the last place went out of business was the money they spent on live music that they couldn't play loud enough or late enough to draw people in from the street. Bar downstairs with a few tables, more tables upstairs on the patio. Kitchen is in a separate building in the back."

"How many walk-in coolers?"

"Three or four. A couple in the kitchen, and then a couple more in a separate, third building, that's in the back to the left. You gonna write any of this down, or you got some sort of secret memory stash."

"I got it, don't worry. What about the other place?"

"Uh-huh, whatever." Now he pulled the toothpick from his mouth and used it as a pointer. "That place, what you see is what you get. The building takes up most of the lot. Seating out front and inside, the main bar is in and to the right, dance floor in the back, kitchen kind of crammed in the far back corner. Upstairs,"

But I didn't need to know what was upstairs. "They have plenty of walk-ins as well?"

"Yeah, sure, I guess." He stood back, eying me over. "Is that what this is? You trying to find a place to store dead bodies?"

"Maybe. Would you like to be the first?"

He smiled the smile of the knowing. "Please. I won't even

Last Pays For All

be the last. Otherwise, you'd have nobody left on this island who'd listen to you." He added with a seriousness that came out of nowhere. "I'm kind of surprised you still have anyone left now."

"You and me both," and that was as maudlin as I was going to allow myself to be. "I think I'm going to go check them out."

"You going to make an appointment with a realtor, or you just planning on inviting yourself in?"

"Inviting myself in." I stood up. "The best parties I've been to are the ones nobody knew I was going to."

"Fair enough. Would you like to know the best way to invite yourself in?"

This information made me sit back down. "Maybe. What do you got for me?"

"The gate that blocks off the back patio of the old Turbo Charged? There's no side to it. You can just climb up and over the half-wall that separates the two properties."

It was my turn to look him over. "And you've done this? Nothing personal, but your size seems to belie that possibility."

"Man, I'm as nimble as a cat. But no, it wasn't me. I used to watch them do it whenever the manager who was supposed to be on duty was too busy sleeping off whatever fun they'd had the night before. Just be careful. Or at least discreet. You might have noticed the people coming and going."

It was hard to miss. Season was still in full bloom, and the cruise ships were still making their daily drop offs. The block was chock full of people coming and going, a steady parade of humanity that unfortunately wasn't stopping often enough to fill Yeddie's tip jar.

Terry

"I know how to make sure nobody's paying attention to me," I explained as I stood back up. "The entire time I'm hopping the wall, I'll be offering everyone free facial treatments if they just step inside my store. That'll make everyone put their eyes down and just keep walking."

"Good luck."

I was going to tell him "Thanks, but I don't think I need it" when my plans came to a screeching halt. I was looking to not draw attention to myself, but somebody else was doing all they could to make everybody notice them.

Why else would you start firing off a gun in the middle of the day?

Last Pays For All

Chapter 15

Several things happen when I hear gunshots go off, and even though I'm going to list them in a 1,2,3 sort of order, believe me when I tell you they all happen at the same time, and that same time is a split second.

The first I do is immediately duck for cover. Without having to think about it, I instantly stepped back and crouched down, allowing the bar to get between me and where the shots were most likely coming from. While this is happening, my right hand is going back to my shorts. Not to find out if anything's been scared out of me, but to get my gun handy. Finally, my ears start working overtime, trying to pinpoint exactly where the shots were fired from and what they might have been fired at.

Yeddie seemed to have none of those instincts. He was still standing up behind the bar. If anything, he moved a little closer to the end towards the street, as if he wanted to be part of the festivities. Both of his hands were on the bar, so he couldn't have been reaching for a gun, not that I think he had one on him. The one thing he was doing though was the most helpful for me.

"From the sounds of it, it's a good thing you didn't try sneaking in there two minutes earlier," he told me. "Whoever's in charge of the property doesn't seem to be wanting any prospective tenants."

I stood up from where I was crouching, enough so I could see the street, scared to say I wasn't quite as fearless as

Terry

Yeddie. People were scattering left and right, screaming was coming from everywhere, and the general panic that the gun person wanted to create was definitely occurring. I kept my ears peaked, listening not only for more gunshots, but also for something else. When I hadn't heard it for about fifteen seconds, I felt a little braver.

"I wonder how many people got hit," Yeddie asked.

"Nobody," I told him. That was what I'd been listening for. There are screams people make when they are panicking, and there are screams people make when they are bleeding. Having heard enough of both of them, I can assure you they don't sound the same. "You'd have heard someone by now if they had been."

"Not if they got killed instantly." You can always count on Yeddie to point out the worst of a bad situation.

"I'm trying to believe that didn't happen, and I have a hunch that it didn't."

"You don't know who your mystery gunman is, but you already know he's a bad shot."

"Not at all. He's probably a very good shot, actually." I moved to the end of the bar. The couple that had been sitting there half a minute ago had already scurried by me on their hands and knees. "I think he wanted to just get some attention."

"Mission accomplished."

"Yeah, but why? And whose?" I had a bad feeling, the same kind of bad feeling I'd been having for the last six weeks. "What do I owe you?"

"It's just getting interesting, and you're leaving?"

"Uh-huh. And I hate to say it, but there's a chance I ain't coming back."

Yeddie seemed shocked to hear such a bold admission on

my part. "In that case, no charge. But if I see you again, twelve-fifty."

"Fair enough." I kept my hand on my gun, but I kept my gun in my shorts. I wanted to be able to get it as quickly as possible, but I also didn't want to risk having it in my hand when the cops showed up. They get a report of gunshots being fired, they come down and see me holding a gun, they probably aren't going to waste too much time asking questions first.

I stepped into the street. The sounds of general panic had subsided into a murmuring buzz that reminded me of the sound you hear under high tension power lines. I was taking a purposeful angle that would draw fire away from the most crowded part of a crowded street, while still allowing myself some level of protection from taking a direct hit. This kept the rest of me from panicking, but part of my brain was showing a montage of movie clips from every western, where the heroic gunslinger crosses the vacant street on his way to shoot it out with the B-list actor in the black hat. My eyes scanned the building, trying to see if I could find the window they had shot through, and occasionally they went the other way, looking to see if I could determine where the bullets had struck. Finally, I ran out of cover, and had no choice but to walk directly in front of the building.

Nothing. I presented as easy a target as possible, but not only did no gun shots ring out, there wasn't even the call of a gun man, making demands and ordering my surrender. It soon became so obvious that nothing else was going to happen that I dared to turn my back to the building and look harder for the ensuing bullet holes.

They were plain as day from this angle. Three shots, perfectly grouped within a few inches of each other, all landing at least a few feet away from where they could have done any damage. They weren't even close enough to a window to shatter some glass with the reverberations of impact. And, from what I could make out from where I was standing, the direction put the shooter up on the second floor, but most likely firing from a prone position.

My shimmying days were long behind me, I thought, but I grabbed onto the nearest column and started to make my way up. I managed to get my hands on the edge of the second-floor porch, secretly thankful that nobody was up there shooting at my fingers or peeling back my nails, when I heard the warning of approaching sirens. Quickly, I dropped back to the ground and made my way back across the street. They might not be as apt to shoot me for breaking and entering as they would be for brandishing a gun, but I wasn't willing to take that chance.

Back at the bar, Yeddie was waiting with his hand out. "That'll be twelve-fifty, please."

Last Pays For All

Chapter 16

Yeddie was laughing as I handed him the money. "You called the cops just to make sure I'd pay my tab."

"I wish, man. But I'm definitely going to have to thank them when they get here."

He went to hand me back the change, but I waved him off. "Well, here's your chance, I think."

"Whaddya mean, you think. They're either cops or they aren't."

"Not when they're sheriffs."

Friend and neighbors, it's time for a little geo-political lesson. Key West is part of Monroe County. In fact, population-wise, it is the biggest part of the county by a wide margin, even if it only takes up the last four miles of a chain that stretches over one hundred and twenty. Because of that, we have our own police force (you may be familiar with some of them by now). A couple of other towns further up the chain have their own squads as well, but a lot of what lays between here and Miami is unincorporated Monroe County. That's where the Sheriffs come into play.

It's not completely uncommon to see the sheriffs in town. They're responsible for patrolling US-1, and there are actually a couple of parcels of county land within the city limits of Key West, but when it comes to things like robberies or drug busts or, I don't know, random gunfire coming from an abandoned restaurant on the middle of Duval Street, they shouldn't be the cavalry that comes rushing in to help.

Terry

One of their squad cars went roaring past the Turbo Charged Café, only to immediately come to a screeching halt directly in front of us. I'm not sure the car had come to a complete stop before the driver bounced out of the vehicle like Tigger from Winnie the Pooh. His head whipped back and forth, ostensibly to be taking in the scene, but I didn't think he'd be able to retain anything he was seeing, seeing how quickly he was moving. Feeling that the area was secured, he used both hands to make sure his hat was probably locked down on his head. Only then did he move to the far side of the car. If he was trying to help his partner out, he was too late.

"I've told you a thousand times, Larson. Save that 'Look at me, Ma, I'm a NASCAR driver' shit for when you aren't on the clock. And I know you're eager to make sure everything here is safe, but maybe next time you don't park the car so your boss is sitting in the potential line of fire." I'm usually not one for first impressions, but this was definitely a guy I knew I was going to like.

"Sorry, sir," Larson said in a voice that sounded anything but. He spoke just as stiffly as he wore his hat. "I was trying to also create a roadblock to keep civilians from coming down this road."

"They'll be quicker to come this way no matter how you're parked if there's the additional dead body of a sheriff lying on the street." By this point he was making his way around the back of the car, and he saw me looking at him while he waved off his deputy. "I've already talked to our local brethren, and they'll be here to take care of traffic."

As if he commanded it to be so, the sound of motorcycle cops approached. Hearing that and not any more gun shots, he decided it was time to start interviewing witnesses. Based on the direction he was walking, me and Yeddie were numbers one and two on that list.

"Morning, gentlemen." He extended a hand to me as he stepped into the shade of the bar. "I'm Officer Davis."

"Pleased to meet you." I shook his hand, but I guess he was hoping for more.

"You got a name?"

I thought for a second. "You good with nicknames?"

"You good with alibis?" he shot back.

"Richard Lockhart." In the end, it didn't matter, because the first name I gave him was just as bullshit as the second one. "But most people call me Tricky Dick."

"That alibi better be getting better," he said, but before I could take him seriously, he winked and continued, "with a nickname like that."

"Edward Callahan, sir."

He shook Yeddie's hand. "Let me guess. You got a nickname, too."

"They call me Yeddie, sir." I probably never would have thought about giggling, but the sheriff had made a potentially tense situation as relaxed as possible. That made the stiffness and nervousness that Yeddie was displaying all the more comical.

"Knew it. Everyone down here has one."

I had to ask, even as I fought to swallow the giggles. "What's yours?"

"They call me the Chatterbox. I'm the hostage negotiator."

Terry

Chapter 17

"We got a call, thirty-five minutes ago. Somebody said they were holding a hostage at this location. They said they had a list of demands, and if there wasn't anyone here to talk to at eleven o'clock, bad things were going to start happening. We missed it by about a minute."

"I don't think you missed much at all." By now there were about ten men, bullet-proof vests on and sidearms in hand, taking up strategic positions around the building. "There were the three gunshots, but that was it. No other sounds, and the shots seemed to have been designed to draw attention but not create carnage."

"That so? You got some experience in this sort of thing?"

Some was all I was willing to concede to. "I managed to make it across the street before you arrived."

"That's a damn foolish thing to do, with a potential active shooter."

"He's a damned foolish type of guy." Whatever childhood experience had made Yeddie seize up in the presence of cops seemed to have evaporated, but I really couldn't disagree with his statement.

"Like you said, I have some experience, and I felt like I had a window of opportunity to find some information, just so I'd have something to tell you when you got here."

He laughed. "You play poker, Tricky?"

"No," wondering what brought this odd segue on.

"Good. Because your face doesn't hide shit. I think you

like me, but you don't much care for the uniform, and my guess is if I hadn't come rolling in when I did, you'd be inside that building right now."

He was a no bullshit type of guy, and I had to respect that. "To be honest, Chatterbox, if I'd known it was you, I probably would have waved to you before I went in."

"With one finger I'm presuming."

"Nah. I save that wave for the asshole I thought you were that kept me from going in the building in the first place."

"Which asshole is that?"

A familiar voice buzzed my ear. "Me."

Terry

Chapter 18

The Mangrove Bar is one of ten bars that sits on this particular piece of property, and when you got that many coolers to fill, shelves to stock, and people to move, you got to have lots of ways for things to come and go. Some of those ways allow people you don't want to be talking to sneak on to the property without being seen, which is exactly what the Chief had done.

"Thanks for getting your boys out to direct traffic, Chief."

"Anything we can do to help, Davis. What's the situation?"

"Hell if I know. We had the one phone call and the one burst of gunfire. Beyond that, nothing. We traced the phone number he called from, and it's definitely inside that building. I've got two units sitting on the back end, just in case he's trying to clip out the back, but for now I'm just waiting for him to call us back."

I had a ton of questions, none of which I had the authority to ask, but I thought them really, really hard, in hopes that the Chief would pick up on them and ask himself.

"What kind of demands did he make in the initial phone call?"

"He didn't. Just said that he had them, but he was saving them for when he could see me while we were talking."

I kept an ear on them as I slid out to take a better look at the building. If the shots had come from the porch, it was also the perfect spot for him to be able to see who he was negotiating with. Problem was, it was also the perfect spot to be seen by people from three different sides, people with guns and a desire to shoot you. I kept looking while the Chief kept asking the right questions.

"How long do you wait to hear from him before you send in the SWAT team?"

"We like to give them at least two hours, but that's if we've had active negotiations that aren't going well. Situations like this, with the gunfire but nothing else, thirty minutes tops, and probably closer to fifteen, in case he's wounding the hostage."

Even if he was, we wouldn't have been able to hear it, considering she was in an airless, soundless room. This information I wanted to share but knew I couldn't, mostly because then I'd have to explain how I knew it in the first place. The Chief checked his watch. "So, at this point, you're thinking another five minutes before you make a move?"

"Hate to do it so quickly, but that's looking to be the scenario." He didn't have to explain just how ready he was for that possibility; the constant chatter on his radio was keeping anybody with a police scanner abreast of their moves. The funny thing was he looked honestly worried about having to send his men in there. The funnier part was how unconcerned the Chief seemed about all of it.

"Cool. That gives us time for a cup of coffee. C'mon Tricky, I'm buying. Davis, you want one?"

If his poker segue earlier was confusing to me, the Chief's offering coffee to him was downright dumbfounding. "Where are you going for coffee?"

"Right there across the street." Chief hiked a thumb over his shoulder. "Their espresso is the best on the island."

"Yeah, I know, I've had it. But, there's a guy with a

gun…"

The Chief just waved him off. "If he hasn't shot yet, he ain't shooting again. So, an espresso it is. We'll be right back." He started across the street, me with no choice but to follow him, and called back to Davis over his shoulder. "Don't start the fun without us!"

Last Pays For All

Chapter 19

I'm not sure where the workers had gone, but I knew where they weren't, so it was up to me to get the coffee. "You really think he's going to raid the place in five minutes?"

"What I think is that in about three minutes he's going to get a call, and that's going to stall him."

"You better be careful. This guy Davis was asking for alibis earlier, and you better start working on yours if you know enough about when phone calls are going to happen."

"It has nothing to do with me. Any professional knows the time parameters and is going to use them to their advantage. This isn't some hothead who's mad his wife is leaving him or angry that the Dolphins still suck. This guy knows what he's doing."

"Yeah? What exactly is that?"

"Distracting us." He took a sip, grimaced, and added about five sugars. "Tell me about the phone call."

"You heard it, you tell me."

"Believe it or not, nobody was listening. I was just concerned about location. It looks bad for the Chief of Police to have a woman he declared dead walking around in society. What the two of you talked about was strictly between you two."

"There wasn't much to tell. We spent the majority of the call determining she was zip tied to a metal chair that was welded to the floor of a walk-in cooler."

Terry

"This explains why you're hanging out around an abandoned restaurant."

"And from the looks of things, I picked the right one. What's our next move?"

"Our move?" There was that damned cocked eyebrow again. "My move is to go back across the street, hand Davis his espresso, and talk to him for as long as possible. I'm sure at some point in the conversation, I'll mention this excitement was just too much for you and you left. As for what your move is, I don't want to know until after you've done it. But from the looks of it, you better do it now."

He pointed across the street. Davis had a phone pressed to his ear with one hand and was tamping down the air with the other, ordering everybody to shut up. Our boy was on the phone, which meant the SWAT team would stand down. Now's the time for me to beat my feet on the Mississippi mud.

"You better be careful, Tricky. You haven't dealt with people like this since you've retired."

"I know." I lifted his flashlight from his utility belt. "Which means they haven't dealt with someone like me, either."

Last Pays For All

Chapter 20

Trust had never been something that ran deep between me and the Chief, even back when we worked together, but I think the demonstration at the police office showed him enough whose side he needed to be on. My days were numbered here, but so were his, and if he wanted them to go smoothly enough so he could accomplish just whatever the hell it was that landed him here in the first place, he was going to have to play nice with me.

At least, that's what I kept telling myself as I ran through the back of the store, trying to convince myself that he wasn't about to shoot me in the back, blame it on the hostage taker, and ride off into the sunset.

I moved through the storeroom (waving politely to the workers who were gathered there and telling them that everything was going to be okay) before scurrying into the back alley that connected the block of buildings in a chaotic, unplanned fashion. I could see where I needed to be, but to get there, I needed to cut through the pool area of a guest house. 'No problem,' I thought to myself. 'These people were probably more skittish than the ones on the street, and the place will be deserted.'

Hardly.

"Can I help you?"

Normally, I would have taken my time to assess the situation covertly, so I could best determine how to slip in and out with nobody seeing me. Wrongly assuming there'd be nobody here to see me, I'd brazenly jumped over the fence, almost landing in some middle-aged blonde woman's Cosmo. Next to her was an older man, snoring away without a care in the world. Beyond him was a group of seven or eight, gathered around a table, chatting away. Or at least they had been, until I arrived.

"No, I'm good, thanks." It was all I could think to say, but she had more in her mouth.

"There is a front door," she gestured casually over her shoulder, "but that's for guests, and I'm guessing you're not really supposed to be here."

"Well, actually ma'am," I knew the word was too old for her, and it brought me a small, cheap thrill to see the sour look run across her haughty face, "I'm on a top-secret government mission that allows me to go wherever I want whenever I need to. So, I'm supposed to be wherever I'm needed. Sorry if that disappoints you."

Maybe it was the brazen way I spoke to her, something I'm sure didn't happen very often, especially from the sleeping slab of flesh next to her, maybe it was the added presence of the gun, something I slid from my shorts while I'd been talking, or maybe she was just bored with life, both specifically today and forever in general, and I was simply the next man she was going to blame. Whatever it was, she warmed up pretty quickly.

"I see. And does that allow you to go inside places whenever you want and wherever you're wanted? A hotel room, for instance?"

"I don't go when I'm wanted. I go when I'm needed."

"I see." She scrolled through her phone, getting out itineraries for her vacation. "Well, the morning after next, he'll be fishing all day. Perhaps then you can find a reason to need to jump over that fence again."

There wasn't a damn thing about her that was less than attractive, so I gave her the best answer I could. "If I'm still alive, I'm sure I can come up with an excuse. Now, if you'll excuse me, you all might want to think about going into your rooms. There's an active shooter in that building right there."

One of the women at the table turned and hit her companion on his arm. "I told you they were gun shots! No truck backfires three times in a row."

"And I told you we didn't have to worry," he replied to her. "The shots didn't come in this direction, and they already have somebody on the scene."

The woman who'd been lied to eyed me up and down coolly, trying to decide if I was professional enough of a savior. I didn't have time to wait for her judgment. I moved down the pool area towards the back wall of the kitchen, thinking that maybe if I got lucky, I'd draw some of his fire this way. The blonde was okay, but a table full of collateral damage might not be the worst thing in the world.

Terry

Chapter 21

Based on what Yeddie had told me, the kitchen was a free-standing building on the back of the property. There were two walk-ins there, a fridge and a freezer. Beyond that, in a little satellite building, were two more, one for bottled beer and another for kegs. It was wishful thinking to only have one, and even more of a fantasy world to believe I'd find her in the first one, but these were the things that kept me going. The more time I spent exploring, the bigger the target I painted on my back.

There was roof damage, most likely left over from last year's hurricane and exasperated by last night's event, that gave me the perfect opening to slide inside the building. Luckily, this put me in between the two walk-ins in the kitchen area. Unluckily, both of them were locked.

The place had been stripped thoroughly clean, the owners taking everything that wasn't nailed down. That didn't give me a lot of hope that I'd find something to cut the locks with, but I owed it to my secrecy and desire to stay alive to at least look for something less noisy than firing a gun at them. A quick run up and down the kitchen line however left me with only a couple of options, both involving items that would only work to break locks by hammering them repeatedly while praying I didn't lose a finger or two in the process. Gunfire it was going to be.

The only thing that had surprised me about the people sitting around the pool – other than that they were there in the first place – was the way they convinced themselves that it had been a truck backfiring. The only people who think a gunshot is a gunshot are people who are used to hearing it on a semi-regular basis. Not even someone who hunts seasonally would think the noise he heard in his neighborhood, while he sat in his chair watching television, was a gun going off. Most people would barely even register it, recognizing it less as a noise and more as something that scared them. If asked, maybe half would be able to properly describe what the noise sounded like, and far fewer would be able to tell where it had come from. But add a second and a third to the first, and suddenly everybody knows what's what.

This was my dilemma. I had to assume the shooter knew somebody was on the property. The Sheriff's department might have its timelines and protocols, but most people wouldn't know what they are. And those smart enough to know them would also be smart enough to plan for any eventuality. I wanted to draw as little attention to myself as possible, which meant not giving him enough time to focus on the gunshots. I pressed the barrel of the gun against one lock and held on to the other.

I didn't look to see how effective my first shot was before swinging the gun and pressing it on the second lock, squeezing the trigger immediately. The powder burns were no fun, neither was the shrapnel of metal shavings that exploded into my hand, but I would worry about that later. The instant the lock disintegrated, I threw it to the floor and whipped open the door, jumping behind it and the safety it offered.

"Rachel?" It was a pointless question; my guess was that if she were in here, she would have already spoken. I'd closed the door, blindly hoping that the emergency exit apparatus was still operational, and clicked on the flashlight.

Nothing. Not a stray lime, an empty six pack holder, a forgotten pallet, nothing. Not even a chair fused to the floor. One down, three to go.

The search across the way was just as effective and empty. I wish I could say it made me feel good that I was at least eliminating possibilities and she was sure to be found in one of the next two, but I'd be lying. Uncertainty has never been my friend, no matter how often it's been part of my life, and I was stepping deeper into it.

From the kitchen door, I could see where the other two walk-ins were. I could also see the edge of the upstairs dining area where the gunman had been shooting from. There wasn't much of a clear shot he could get on me between here and the walk-in door, but the roofing material wasn't enough to stop anything stronger than a Daisy air rifle. Once again assuming he had an idea of where I was on the property, I had to chance it. I thought about finding a stray rock or brick and throw it at the stairs leading up to him, hoping to cause a distraction, but decided it was pointless. The best way to stay alive in situations like this is to believe the person you're up against is a genius, or at least a professional. Some amped out guy with a gun making irrational demands would pull the trigger at any stray sound he heard. A professional will fire not at where the object ended up, but where it started off.

The third walk-in was five giant steps away, but thankfully unlocked. I refused to allow myself to think if this was a good or bad sign, and instead focused on where to step when and which way the door opened. Decision made, I didn't take any time to second guess myself.

Last Pays For All

The door swung open wide, and even though it moved away from the opposite wall, blocking most of the natural light, enough snuck through that I could see everything that was in the room without using the flashlight.

A welded chair, a bunch of cut zip ties, and a dead cell phone.

Wherever she was now, she wasn't where she had been.

Terry

Chapter 22

I want to say I had a calm, rational reaction to this discovery. You should know me well enough by now to know that something like that isn't wishful thinking. I'd like to think (wouldn't we all?) that, more often than not, my reactions have been measured and well executed. Yeah, I guess ramming a bag full of fishing weights into a man's nuts or shooting a cop in the throat might not seem like the most rational things to do, but I'd like to think of those as the exceptions, and not the rule.

Now was time for an exception. I had no way of contacting the Chief or the Sheriff if I wanted to, and the only person who had answers for me now was somewhere on the second floor. Or at least, he had been. If he took off with her after he'd fired the gun, he could have slipped away, and even though a ten-minute head start doesn't sound like a lot, it is typically more than enough. I wasn't in the mood to give him eleven minutes.

I rushed up the back stairs, sliding on the floor when I reached the landing. The wood frame of the old building wouldn't be much cover, but it'd be more than the wall of windows above it. I peeked my head up. Through the dusty glass, there was nothing to see. I mean that. Nothing. A few leftover U-Haul boxes that they put together but didn't need for the move, and that was it. The pool table, the high tops, the stools, all of it was gone.

I crawled to the front balcony, and when I looked around

the corner, I finally saw something important. The barrel of a gun, facing out, was wedged under the front door. I didn't have to get any closer to know exactly where it was aiming. Pull the trigger a hundred times and there'd be a four-inch starburst pattern on the building opposite us, right where the first three bullets had landed.

I scuttled back to where I had originally landed on the porch. The door inside was locked, but seeing as nobody seemed to be around, I didn't think anyone would care if I broke my way in. Careful not to slit my wrist open on the broken glass, I fumbled for the handle and let myself in. The random boxes that had been left behind suddenly didn't seem so random anymore, but instead piled together in such a way to keep some things hidden. I could see the stock end of the rifle, and from the trigger were a couple of wires running into the box closest to it.

Upon further inspection, it appears I spoke too soon when I said trigger. It had been removed and replaced with what looked like a fuse box of some sort, a conduit designed to turn an electrical signal into a physical act. I began tracing it back to the box when I was distracted by the sound of a phone ringing, coming from the larger of the two boxes.

Inside was a laptop with the printed text, not only of a previous conversation, but of what was happening now. Literally. I could read the words "ring", "ring", "ring." I probably would have read a fourth one, but somebody answered.

"This is Davis. Glad you're back."

As he spoke, his voice unmistakable, his words appeared on the screen, as did the response.

"Call me old fashioned, but I like to piss in private."

The voice was normal, natural, human. In other words,

nothing that would distinguish it as being a preprogrammed computer sequence.

"I wouldn't call you anything. But I would like to ask you some things."

"Shoot." The voice laughed. "Well, don't shoot, but, you know what I mean."

"I don't want anyone to shoot, and that includes you."

"I don't want to shoot either, so please don't give me any reason to."

"I'm trying not to, but for that to happen, we need to come to some understanding. The first one being why you're doing this."

My fascination with reading the conversation in real time expired, so I just listened to the early stages of a negotiation as I went back to the first box. Here was another tablet, sitting on top of a roughly shoebox sized item, and wired between it and the gun was something that looked like a kid's project from the back of Popular Mechanics. I didn't need to be an engineer to know it converted whatever the tablet told it into the electrical impulse to fire the gun. This tablet wasn't talking to anyone; instead it just had a series of timers. The first one was at 0:00, the third one read 1:10, the fourth, 1:58, and the fifth, in a different color, 3:15. It was the second timer, the one that was running backwards, that interested me. It was at just about twenty minutes now, and some quick deducing on my part told me that's how much time was left before it began shooting again.

My first reaction was to simply disable the contraption somehow. Maybe just pull the wires, smash the tablet or disarm the gun, but then I remembered that I had to expect I was dealing with a professional. The same professional who would assume I was coming in here to rescue Rachel would

Last Pays For All

also assume I would make my way up here. The last thing he would want was me tampering with his handiwork, and if I did, I think it was that shoebox looking thing that would have something to say to me. Thankfully, I had twenty minutes and counting to do something about it.

I made my way down the inside steps towards the front door. The windows here were just as dusty as the ones upstairs, but I could see through them clearly enough to count the number of men with weapons trained on the building. There would be no smashing of windows and forcibly opening doors now, not if I wanted to keep my blood where it belonged. Thankfully, this door had been sealed with an interior deadbolt, one that was easy enough for me to dismantle. Slowly, I nudged the door open, being sure to put two hands up as soon as I could get them outside.

I saw every man tense up and train their focus on me, but I was most concerned with catching Davis's eye. Thankfully I did right as I saw him hesitate on the phone. That couldn't happen.

"You!" I yelled, pointing at him. "Keep talking like I'm not here. And you," I pointed at the Chief, "Get over here now."

Davis listened like the pro he was, and the Chief crossed the street, one eye fixed on me and the other looking up at the porch. Safely underneath it, he finally spoke.

"I wasn't sure I could trust you not to get me shot."

"I wasn't sure either. My computer knowledge is pretty limited, but I think I have enough of an understanding of what's going on. Follow me."

As I led him up the stairs, I described the empty walk-in I had found and what had been left behind. He might have had questions but knew better than to ask them until he had all the information. Upstairs, we watched and listened to the conversation between the Chatterbox and the computer. Finally, he spoke.

"It must be one hell of a program, if it's able to have a script that it can force Davis to follow."

"I think it's more than that. I don't think it cares what gets talked about, just as long as it keeps him talking, when it wants him to."

"What do you mean, when?"

I pointed out the second tablet. "It needs to fire the gun at those appointed times, just to keep things moving at the pace it wants to. Basically, it wants to keep us here for another three hours, while whoever's behind this has time to get Rachel where they want her for good."

He let out a low whistle. "Guess I shouldn't be surprised by the level of sophistication."

"You got anyone on your staff who's a cracker jack with computers?"

"Yeah, but I also got guys who are good with a sledge hammer."

"Careful, Chief. Computers are dainty things. I'd rather we know for sure what we're up against. Besides, maybe there's more information on here that we could use."

Last Pays For All

Chapter 23

We spent the next fifteen minutes watching one of his guys, a cadet who should probably carry his ID for the next five years anytime he went to a bar just to be sure he'd get served, play around on the computer. I'm not even going to pretend to understand what he was doing or what he was looking for, so all I'll say is the negotiation continued on unabated, and there was probably no fewer than six times the Chief and I tensed up at the thought that whatever he was trying was going to end both badly and quickly. Finally, he stopped and told us very excitely what we needed to know.

"It's an almost completely self-contained system. There's a Wi-Fi connection, but the only thing it's using that for is to keep the phone call going."

The Chief stopped him right there. "So, he's actually talking to a computer and not a person?"

"Exactly."

"How?"

"The only program that's on the computer, other than a basic operating system, is some sort of algorithm and a very healthy alphabet. It's basically a low rent version of artificial intelligence that's keeping the conversation running. The other tablet is even less, just the timers."

"Does it matter that the two tablets are connected?"

"Yes, but I'm not sure how much. It could be the battery on the larger one is powering both, or it could be some level of communication, making sure that they work together."

"Can we cut the cord, between the tablet and the gun, so it doesn't fire anymore?"

"I don't see why not. It's a one-way connection. The tablet sends a message to this box, the box converts it to an electrical impulse, and the impulse triggers the firing mechanism. As long as the tablet stays connected to the box, it thinks it's doing its job. It never knows whether the gun fires or not, nor does it care."

The Chief wanted confirmation on his original assessment. "That sounds like a pretty sophisticated piece of equipment." But the kid wasn't impressed.

"Well, it's not just something you'd put together from a kit in the back of Popular Mechanics," (shit!) "but it's also nothing too elaborate. They easily could have designed something far more advanced, including fail safes for a situation like this."

"So why didn't they?" I was asking the kid, but the Chief felt like responding.

"Because they assumed that the Sheriff would be in control of the situation. In a hostage situation, everything falls in line behind whoever is doing the negotiating, and they felt comfortable enough to think that would include us."

Now it was the kid's turn to ask a question. "Why wouldn't it?"

"Never mind that. What's the box it's sitting on?"

"I'm not sure." He wasn't, but I could tell by the way he said it, he had a pretty good guess and I asked him why that was.

"It's wired directly into the tablet, meaning any disconnect would be recognized immediately. And the box isn't connected to anything else, meaning it has no say in the firing of the gun or the continuation of the conversation."

"Meaning we should probably get the bomb squad in here."

He sheepishly nodded his head. I checked the timer. "You sure about being able to cut the wires?"

"Pretty sure."

"That's gonna have to be sure enough for me. Give me your knife."

"What are you doing?"

"Something we only have about ninety seconds left to do, unless we want more gunfire."

The Chief suddenly had doubts about something. "Are you sure that's what the timer is for?"

"It isn't just the timer. Haven't you been listening to the conversation between the computer and the Chatterbox?"

"There isn't one right now."

"That's my point."

The kid had moved to look at the computer, and he was speed reading half aloud the last several exchanges. "Yeah, it sounds like he's getting ready to shoot. 'You're not taking me seriously.' 'Do you think this is a joke?' 'I guess I need to do something other than talk.' That was the last thing he said."

I threw up my hands and cocked my head to the side, the international sign of "See? I told you so!" in the direction of the Chief.

"Give them a cut."

"Ummm, wait a second." Now it was the kid's turn to have doubts, but I knew exactly what his were.

"Start running. But if we don't blow up in the next twenty seconds, get your ass back up here."

"Why?"

"To help us figure out what we're going to do with the bomb."

Last Pays For All

Chapter 24

The kid double timed it down the back stairs as I knelt over the gun. Can't say as I blame him. He's still young with lots of life left in front of him. The Chief and I, well, I'm not saying we're old, but there ain't much left in the world we haven't experienced.

"Which one are you cutting first?"

"I'm not." I sliced through them both at the same time. Despite the rubber grip on the knife, I could still feel a bit of a shock in the palm of my hand. The timer on the tablet wasn't like every single movie you've ever seen; instead of dramatically stopping with fractions of a second left, it simply ran to zero, the other ones continuing their own count. But beyond that, nothing happened.

I slid the gun out from under the door to get a better look at it. "Belong to anyone you know?" the Chief asked me.

"Probably, but the list of people shooting at me is pretty extensive. Still, there's one way to know for sure."

I popped out the magazine, partially to see how many shots had been planned, but mostly to see if somebody left a signature. Sure enough they did.

I tossed one of the bullets to the Chief. "Look familiar?"

"Same writing on the shells we pulled off of Rachel's body."

"Who's body?"

"Rachel's." He was committed to the lie, but not me.

"If that was Rachel, what are you doing here?"

He had to think about it for a moment, not because he

didn't know what the answer was, but to find the right words to express it with. "I'm not saying I don't trust you to tell me the truth behind all of this when you finally figure it out. I'm just saying I'd like to see as much of it with my own eyes as I possibly can." Having shared enough emotion with me for the time being, he turned his attention back to the bullet. "Don't let the Cyrillic alphabet throw you off. Everything Russian is cheap these days, especially ammunition. They could be using it as much as an identifying mark for your benefit as they are because they got three boxes for a dollar at last week's black market tag sale."

"I think it's somewhere in between." I was debating on whether to tell him more, halfway assuming he already knew what my information was, when the kid came back up the stairs.

"I'm guessing it's okay to come back."

"We're both still here, so I guess that's a good sign."

He took another look at the tablets. The smaller one caught his eyes "Huh. I didn't think that would happen."

"What?"

"That all the timers would stop."

"They didn't."

"You sure about that?"

The Chief and I looked into the box. Sure enough, the remaining timers were frozen, flashing the numbers they had paused at. I hadn't committed the remaining time to memory when I looked after cutting the wires, but I was comfortable enough with my recollection to guess they had run about ten more seconds or so before stopping. The question was why.

"The bigger question," the Chief posed, as if he was

reading my mind, "is what happens when they start running again?"

"I guess the same thing they were designed to do in the first place."

"You guess?"

"Hey, this isn't exactly the type of computer science they covered in the Academy." The kid had spunk, I'll give him that. "They may not even restart at the same time."

"Why wouldn't they?"

"Because nobody's talking to it." It suddenly dawned on me what was going on. The gun should have fired almost a minute ago by now, and the computer program was waiting for a response from the Sheriff. If there was an open line of communication, it would be the logical thing to do. If.

"Is there any way to see if the phone call between the two is still connected?" I asked the kid. There must have been some panic in my voice because he moved quickly.

"No. It's been disconnected for two and half minutes now."

When I had moved the gun from the door, I'd done so as discreetly as possible. Any movement up here might trigger a response from down there. I was still worried about them shooting first, but now I was more worried about the building exploding. The computer might have a back-up plan, that once the communication between the two was cut off for a certain period of time, it would just trigger the explosion, and I wasn't in the mood to find out if I was right.

I ran at the door, and the hinges went just as quickly as the deadbolt. I almost tripped over what was left of the door as I reached onto the railing and flipped myself over. I took a flash of a second to look as I went ass over teakettle, lining up my drop zone. Luckily, the owner had been meticulous about taking everything with him, so the front bar area was spotless. What saved me from being shot when I jumped was the brazenness with which I moved. I don't think anyone was expecting such a departure, and I had to give them credit for having calm heads and cool trigger fingers. What saved me from being shot when I landed was what I started yelling.

"Don't shoot! Don't shoot! It's me! It's me!!" I ran across the street directly to Davis. "You got a phone number for your guy?"

"Yeah."

"Call him now, right now, and the first thing you say, regardless of whatever he says when he picks up the phone, is 'I had to wait a minute to call you, just to let my blood stop boiling. You want to tell me why you shot at us?'"

He hit the redial button. "But he didn't shoot at us."

"Believe me, he thinks he did. Just say it."

From the other end of the phone, I heard the computer pick up. Thankfully, he had the perfect opening line. "What took you so long?"

Davis looked at me and I mouthed his words to him. "I had to wait a minute to call you, just to let my blood stop boiling. You want to tell me why you shot at us?"

"Because I didn't think you were taking me seriously."

"We certainly are now, even though we always have been. So, let's talk some more."

I walked over to the Mangrove Bar, where Yeddie continued to have a front row seat for all the festivities. Instinctively, he handed me a beer.

"Thanks, but I actually need a pen and a piece of paper." He went to move the beer away, but I stopped him. "I didn't say I didn't want it."

Last Pays For All

In the time it took him to scrounge up some paper and a pen, I'd finished half the beer. The other half disappeared while I wrote down short-term instructions for Davis, which consisted mostly of telling him to keep the guy talking until further notice. I handed it off to him and, much to the alarm of all the deputies, walked back inside the restaurant.

"Kid, you got two choices. You can hang out here with us while we discuss several things, ranging from who's on the bomb squad to why a collection of mercenaries wants me dead, captured or both, or you could head downstairs, and keep your mouth shut about what's going on up here." The kid's response was perfect.

"I don't think either option is really good for me. I think any good option I had went out the window when I came inside this building."

I knew what he was trying to say, but for some reason the Chief didn't. "What do you mean?"

"I'm not really sure why you're here, how long you're staying, where the old chief went, or what's really going on. All I know is you're bad news, every good cop knows it, and now that I'm stuck in the middle of some elaborate lie, they're going to think the same of me. Thanks to you, my career's over in this town, before it ever really got started. What I should do is go downstairs and tell anybody who would listen exactly what's going on up here, but something tells me if I do that, I might want to make sure my life insurance is paid up first."

I never in my life have felt bad for the Chief, but if I were ever going to, now would be the time. The kid had laid out the situation perfectly. His career was over, because there was no way he could wash the odor of taint away that the Chief visited on him simply because of his computer knowledge. What made me almost feel bad was the fact that I could see the Chief was affected by the kid's words.

"You're probably right, pretty much across the board. There are things going on that are far bigger than this department, far bigger than this town. It's the perfect situation of wrong place, wrong time, not just for you, but for Key West itself. Because of that, there are things happening that I wouldn't be proud to be a part of, if I had any pride in the first place. You, however, have that pride, and that's important. It'll be more important in the next couple of days, believe me. The best thing you can do is take Tricky's second suggestion, walk out of here, and stand down for the next forty-eight hours. Head out of town, go visit friends, whatever, and when you come back to work after that, you'll see where that pride comes in handy."

The kid looked us both over, seeing if he could gauge the honesty of what the Chief had said. "And you trust me to not say anything about this to anyone?"

The iciness of the words that came from the Chief officially eliminated any chance of me having empathy for him. "I'll know the minute it happens if it does, and I'll take care of it one minute later."

The kid took those words to heart and started for the interior staircase when I stopped him. "For everyone's comfort, take the outside stairs, cut through the kitchen, hop the fence, and walk off into the sunset. That way, you won't be asked a million questions by the Sheriff." He was about to follow my lead when I grabbed him by his arm. "And if you see a blonde by the pool, late thirties, stacked, tell her our date is still on."

Last Pays For All

Chapter 25

The Chief and I headed down the stairs and out the front door. As a matter of precaution, I kept my hands above my head; the Chief figured the uniform he was wearing would preclude anyone from shooting him. I caught Davis's eye again and gave a rolling over finger motion. He ok'd me and did exactly what I wanted him to: kept talking. Chief radioed for his bomb squad to roll in, and I did what I did best.

"Glad to see this retirement is treating you well."

"Thanks, Yeddie. I just think of all the extra social security benefits I'm accruing."

"Am I in any danger of getting shot anytime soon?"

"Shot? No. That's not going to be a problem."

He regarded me for a second. "Uh-huh. I'm not exactly sure you told me I was perfectly safe, though."

"You're hanging out with me. How safe is anyone in that situation?"

The Chief came back over. "The van will be here in five minutes. What do we do in the meantime?"

"Same thing we're going to do after they get here. Sit around and wait. Whoever's behind this was nice enough to give us a timeline. We've got about three hours before the bomb is set to go off. That gives us time to plan."

"For what? Not sure if I missed it, but there wasn't a whole lot in the way of clues up there."

"There doesn't have to be, because we don't have to stay

here. Follow me." I led him over to where Davis was, and, in a display that looked more like a third base coach giving signals to the batter than a bad attempt at sign language, I got him to understand that I wanted him off the phone for two minutes.

"Hey, it's my turn to answer nature's call. Would you like to talk to my partner, or should I just call you back?"

There was a pause, and my thought was that this question wasn't one it expected, so it had to work out an answer. "Let me talk to your partner. Maybe he'll tell me some of your secrets."

Davis forced a laugh, trying to keep everything congenial. "Let's hope he doesn't. Hold on a second." He handed the phone off to the other negotiator, who winked as he started speaking.

"So, what would you like to know about him?"

"C'mon," Davis said. "I really do gotta pee, so let's walk and talk."

I wasn't thrilled to have to follow him to the men's room, but I wanted to have as much time as possible with him, because I wasn't convinced he was going to be buying what I was selling. As much as I liked his no-nonsense approach to things, I discovered he was allowed to live that way because, ultimately, he ran things by the book, and nothing about this situation was ever found in any chapter he'd ever read.

"You're telling me I'm talking to nobody? That nothing's going on up there?"

"Pretty much."

"And tell me again, then, why we're wasting our time doing this?"

"Because there may be a bomb up there, and if it is, it may

be wired to a fail-safe thing, so maybe if we stop the communication, call it out, it..."

"It maybe blows up the whole block."

"Something like that, maybe, yeah."

He turned to the Chief, as much to ask him why I was even involved in this as to find out what his thoughts were.

"We've got the bomb squad on the way. Once they take a look at it, tell us what we're dealing with and how we can disable it, we'll know what our next several moves can be."

"And in the meantime, you're sure there's nobody in there."

"As sure as I can be. I didn't check out every nook and cranny, but I was in pretty much the entire building and didn't see anyone."

"Pretty much the entire building, or the entire building?"

"Pretty much. I didn't go into the downstairs interior."

"Mm-hmm." He waved behind him, and a deputy who was waiting to do one specific thing showed up to complete his task, handing Davis a schematic of the building. "That unexamined interior includes two bar rooms, a retail shop, a walk-in closet and two bathrooms. Ample place for a person to be hiding. And you want me to believe there's nobody in there."

My answer was going to be something along the lines of "If there was, don't you think they would have shot me already, since I fucked with their little happy homewrecker automatic gun kit?" but luckily, the Chief was possessing a cooler head.

"Right now, we have forty-four minutes and twenty seconds before he is supposed to shoot again. When that time comes, if that's what happens, will you believe us?"

"Ummm, Chief, that's a good plan, but you're forgetting

something."

"Yeah, that you supposedly disabled the gun."

"Nothing supposed about it. That gun ain't going to fire. But right before it should, you'll hear the guy you're talking to start to make more demands, irrational ones. You'll hear him display signs of anger and frustration, and he'll try to assert his dominance, no matter what you do. And no matter what you do, he'll 'fire' his gun in forty-four minutes. If that happens?"

"If that happens, we'll do things your way. In the meantime, we'll do things my way."

"Except for the bomb squad."

Davis rolled his eyes. "Yes, except for the bomb squad." He shook his head, feeling, I'm sure, much like our hacker cadet had: no matter how much training you have, there are some things you are just never prepared for. He waved again, and his partner handed him the phone.

"I'm back. Did I miss anything important?"

"Nothing exciting. Took you a while."

"I was washing my hands." He said the next thing loud enough for the Chief and I to hear it. "I like to be as clean as possible when I'm dealing with a dirty situation"

Last Pays For All

Chapter 26

Forty-two minutes later, Davis was having an almost pointless conversation with a person who didn't exist, I was playing Yeddie rummy for my bar tab, and the bomb squad was telling the Chief so many things that he didn't want to hear, which could be summed up in one phrase:

"We have no idea what it is, so we ain't fucking with it."

The best they could do, which would turn out to be the only thing they would do, is to place a containment cap over it. I can't imagine there are many things that are more unpleasant than wearing forty pounds of protective body armor while carrying a sixty pound piece of lead up a flight of stairs on a ninety degree day with similar humidity, but that's the glamourous life they signed up for. The downside to the way the cap was put together were the seams at the corners. They still offered protection, but obviously not as much. The good thing about those bad seams was that it allowed the phone call to continue unabated. Once they had finished building their little bomb cave, they did what the rest of us were doing: sitting and waiting.

I drew another card, spiked my discard upside down on the pile, and laid out my last run. "Son of a bitch."

"Don't worry. I wasn't really going to make you pay my tab."

"You might as well. I ain't going to make any money anyway. Police actions aren't good for business."

"That's why you gotta keep whatever you can." I stood

up to stretch and light a cigarette, when I saw Davis waving towards me and the Chief. I thought the guy waved an awful lot, but I guess silent communication comes in handy when you're trying to convince a coked out, soon-to-be ex-husband not to shoot his wife before your boys can get in there.

When we got within earshot, we could hear the conversation we were expecting. "That's not what I said at all...no, you're misunderstanding what I said...no, I'm not calling you stupid...yes, I understand that you are capable of hurting her, and us, and I don't want it to come to that...no, I'm not doubting you...hello? Hello?" He looked at the dead phone. "Hung up."

The Chief checked his watch. "Right on time." He must have set alarms to tie in with the countdowns on the tablet, because fifteen seconds later his watch started beeping.

"What do I do now?"

"Call him right away," the Chief instructed. "Compliment him on proving his point."

"And then?"

"I'm still trying to figure that out." We stepped back from everyone else for our own conversation.

"Why not just storm the place now?"

The Chief shook his head. "The bomb squad boys have given me no assurances that the device can't have any number of fail-safes that would detonate it prematurely."

"It didn't when we were up there, nor when the squad contained it."

"Which makes me think everything up there is more advanced than we thought."

Meaning that whoever was pulling the strings from wherever they were, might know the difference between the

Last Pays For All

Chief and I and everybody else. They still might need us for whatever they were trying to prove. There was obviously a bounty on my head, or at least what some people believed was inside it, and scattering that all over Duval Street would not be the best way to access it. Blowing up a SWAT team, or a bunch of deputies, however, would go a long way towards driving public opinion in a bad direction, one in which the Chief already seemed to be taking the police department. Of course, there was no way to know for sure that was true; the SWAT team could storm the place, prove it's clear of people, and the bomb could just keep on ticking away. That was just it: even if didn't explode on the siege, it would still explode eventually, a point I brought up with the Chief.

"I was afraid that whatever we were dealing with was more than whatever they'd dealt with, so I made another phone call."

"Boca Chica?"

"Yup." There's an advantage sometimes to having a large military presence in your backyard. You had the best Fourth of July parades, you got free air shows on an almost daily basis, and, when you needed someone who had experience dealing with obscure and advanced explosives usually only found in foreign wars and shady black markets, they were usually just a short phone call and shorter ride away. In the meantime, it was more of the same: hurry up and wait.

With nothing better to do, we went back to Davis. Since we had seemingly proved ourselves right, he embraced talking to a computer in a new way. The formality he'd been using before had gone to the wayside, and much like his request to use the restroom had thrown off the computer, the new tone and cadence he was employing made the computer slower on the responses and sounding almost defensive. The Chief wasn't as amused by it as I was, and I motioned for the phone.

"Hold on for a second. I gotta take care of something, but there's someone else who wants to talk to you."

The Chief shot me a worried look at Davis handed me the phone, but I brushed him off. "Don't worry. What's the worst that can happen?" I rolled the cigarette to the corner of my mouth. "Good morning. How you doing today?"

Pause. "Yes, good morning, at least for a little bit. I'm fine, how are you?"

"I've been better, to be honest. You're kind of fucking my day up."

Pause. "Yes, I am. Sorry about that." Another pause. "Who is this?"

"Just a friend of the negotiator. And the Chief."

Pause. "The police chief?" But before I could answer, it did. "Oh yes, you are. I recognize your voice now. Hold on a moment."

The air went dead on the phone. Davis, who'd been listening, joined the Chief in the worried look department. "In almost two hours, he never asked me to hold on. He either talked, told me to call back in a certain time, or just hung up."

"What can I say? I have a way with people."

The dead air was replaced with the sound of a phone ringing. Whatever program was running the computer was now putting that Wi-Fi signal to an even better use. After three rings, somebody answered, and said the two words none of us wanted to hear.

"Hello, Tricky."

The voice was familiar enough to stick in my head, but not so much that I knew who I was talking to. Part of it was the context. Whoever it was, I'd never spoken to them over the phone before and only in person, that much I knew. Part of it was also the rush of noise in the background. I had to work hard in the short silence I allowed myself between speaking to try and identify it.

"Well, this is awkward. You knowing me, but me not knowing you."

"Don't kid yourself. We both know you know me, and we both know you can't place me right now. But, I bet I can place you."

"Oh yeah?" I asked, somewhat stupidity. "Where do you think that might be?"

"You're downtown, sitting at one of your many favorite bars with one of your many favorite bartenders, looking at one of your favorite vacant buildings."

Thank God evil people love to hear themselves talk. The more he talked, the more I could figure out. There were three things working together to make the sound that muffled his voice: wind, waves, and horsepower. He was somewhere on a boat, and I had to assume she was somewhere on that boat with him. He continued.

"I heard from a friend that you're interested in opening your own bar down here. Kind of a strange way for you to waste your money, but if that's what you want, let me help you make a decision."

"How are you going to do that?" And how did he know what I was talking to Scarlett about? Was she one less person that I could trust, or one more person I needed to check in on?

"By convincing you to buy this property. You'll do it out of guilt, because you'll believe it's your fault I did this to it."

And before I could see and feel the explosion across the

street from me, I heard it rushing at me through the earpiece of the phone.

Last Pays For All

Chapter 27

"On the bright side, he can install a fireman's pole right here. Be a fun way for people to get back down to the first floor."

I guess when you work in ordinance disposal, you develop a rather off-beat sense of humor. I could tell that the Chief wanted to engage that thought, pointing out things such as liability insurance, lawsuits, and busted ankles, but instead he pinched the bridge of his nose, as if he could push the thought into oblivion, and walked away. I knew enough to follow him.

"I'm guessing there's no hope in that call being traced."

"If there was, the computer that could help us is in about a million different pieces. Did you pick up on anything that he said?"

I had, but I wasn't going to tell the Chief that. Let me figure out on my own whose side Scarlett was playing on. "Nothing he said stood out. But I could tell that he was on a boat, moving at a fair clip, so that's something."

The Chief looked at me with the same expression of incredulity he'd given the stand-up bomb squad guy. "We're an island, Tricky. Water, water everywhere, and not a place to search."

"Just because you're willing to accept that she's dead doesn't mean I have to."

"It might." We sat down on a wall at the corner of the block as fire department vehicles started to leave the area, allowing pedestrians back on the block. "For starters, you don't know that she's with him on the boat. He could have arranged the phone call, and then killed her."

"No, he couldn't have."

"You're not facing reality, Tricky."

"Chief, you're not. If they kill her, what's the incentive for me to stick around? I'm the prize in all of this. Scooter learned to do something none of us have done, and not only did he use it to his own advantage, he managed to piss off some pretty heavy hitters along the way. Now for some reason, those people think I can do the same thing, and they want me to go back and clean up Scooter's mess, or at least teach them how to do it. And if they ain't giving me a reason to come find them, none of that's ever going to happen."

He mulled that over. "Are you sure she's the biggest bargaining chip that they have with you?"

"Biggest chip? Hell, she's the only chip." And she was, for reasons I couldn't begin to figure out. I'd been a very happy and successful love 'em and leave 'em bachelor during my retirement years, making up for the work-imposed celibacy I'd been living with during those earlier years. I know that doesn't make me a candidate for "Gentleman of the Year", but it was a lifestyle I enjoyed and, more importantly, could handle. Emotional entanglements – well, there you go, the fact that I refer to them as something to be tangled up in should tell you everything you need to know – were not things I needed in my life. Yet somehow, Rachel had become one. There was a concern I felt for her that didn't make sense to me.

"You sure about that?"

"Who else do I have in my life, Chief? You? They could take you, and I'd draw up the map leading them out of

Last Pays For All

town."

"Maybe it isn't just the people in your life now you should be concerned about."

"Don't even think about that." I certainly wasn't going to. Instead, I stood up and paced, lighting a cigarette. The Chief wasn't about to follow my advice.

"You don't know even if he's still alive, do you?"

"No, and I don't want to. Get that?" The Chief did. He knew everything about him, starting from the moment I walked out the door on his first day of kindergarten. "I made peace with my decision years ago, and part of making that peace was creating my own world of truth, a world where he's dead, and I can't do anything about it."

"But, what if?"

"He's not!" I was in his face. "And if you're trying to tell me he is, and that someone else has found him, hell's going to be paid for by lots of people."

"All I'm trying to tell you," he spoke to me in a calming tone, one he'd been trained to use by psychologists to soothe unsuspecting people into revealing inappropriate facts, "is that you have to understand there are other pieces out there that you need to consider. Because they might be, if they aren't already."

"But you still can't tell me she's dead."

"I'll tell you what I have to. What you choose to do with that information is up to you." A monstrous yawn escaped me. "When was the last time you slept?"

"Night before last." And during this time of being awake, my body had been healing from a fine number of unnatural ailments.

"You aren't going to choose to do anything clearly until you get some sleep. Let's go."

"I can walk to my dinghy from here."

"You're not going to your dinghy."

"Are you arresting me?"

"I should. It would help put things right in the eyes of a lot of people on this island. But I can't vouch for your safety when you're alone in your cell."

"Where can you vouch for it?"

"Back at my house."

If you're thinking this is a funny turn of events from what had been going down between the Chief and I most recently, you ain't the only one laughing. Six hours ago, I threatened to kill him, and he basically returned the offer, and now he was telling me I should go to his place, under the guise of safety? I wasn't stupid enough to think there wasn't an ulterior motive behind it, but I also wasn't smart enough to think of a reason to say no. There was only one thing I could say as we walked to his car.

"I can't sleep long. I still gotta find Rachel."

And he knew better than to say anything.

Last Pays For All

Chapter 28

Either the Chief had been watching a lot of home design shows over the last few years, or the house he rented came fully furnished, because there was no way he could have been bothered to take the time to do such a good job laying the house out, much less know exactly what colors worked with what, and which pieces of furniture would be best. I still wasn't convinced he had my best interests at heart, and I told him so.

"I don't mostly. Think of this as house arrest. I want to keep an eye on you. I know you want to go out there, but in the condition you're in, there's no way you'll be any good to me."

"To you?"

"To me," he confirmed. "You may hate the thought of this, but you're my pawn in this game."

"I'm starting to feel like everyone's pawn."

"That's not a bad way to look at it."

"So, tell me then. If I'm stuck here with you, at least give me the courtesy of telling me why I'm so important to you."

He poured himself a coffee and me a whiskey, probably afraid the caffeine would do for me what the booze wouldn't. "Everybody out there, at least everybody we know about, knows something about what Scooter did. We know the theory of what he did, but we can't figure out exactly what it was. There's no way to trace his steps. Not only did he change things, he then erased it, so for us, there's no way to know what that event was. All we know is how he did it."

"Something none of us were supposed to be able to do."

"Well...yes." His hesitation told me he knew exactly how it had been done, that it wasn't as impossible as we'd been led to believe, and he wasn't about to confirm any of that for me. "That's the tricky part on our side. Don't take this personally, but we know you can't do it."

"My ego's taken bigger hits."

"But these other people, they don't know that. They think you have the same ability Scooter has."

"And that's it? That's why they want me?"

"That's hardly it. It would be, if there were only two interested parties involved. But there are several others, who simply want the technology we have. They think you can provide that."

"Why not just let me tell them I can't?" I was half joking when I said that, but he was all serious when he answered.

"Because you can. Nobody's figured out how to have you tap into it yet, is all." He was done revealing company secrets. "There's a spare bedroom at the end of the hall. Make yourself comfortable."

"I'll be comfortable when I find Rachel."

"You're like a dog with a stick. Can't just let it go."

"Not if she's alive out there, and in trouble."

"Believe me, as long as she's alive, the person in trouble is you."

I had to remember that he had a working relationship with her, one that was far different, and far more suspect, than mine. I wanted to ask him more, but I knew he was done talking for the day, so I got up and headed for the hallway. "What are you going to do while I get my beauty sleep?"

He laughed. "Probably start updating my resume. I'm pretty sure I'm going to be out of a job soon."

Terry

Chapter 29

The Chief was trying to do me a favor, and my body appreciated it, but my mind had other things on its...well, you know. With nothing else to do, it could finally start to work out the loopholes that had been troubling me just a short time ago.

Whatever Rachel and I almost started to have between us fell apart by the time we got back from Bimini. We certainly made continual stabs at it over the ensuing few weeks, but it became obvious, at least to me, that the trust issue was never going to be resolved. Each of us were hiding more than just a separate bank account and a jealous ex. Normally, none of that would've bothered me, because none of it would've mattered. Ian Fleming didn't create the sex life James Bond displayed as much as to just report it to the masses. There have been plenty of times I'd been deep on assignment, and the only woman I found attractive who found me the same was the woman I knew I should least trust, and she knew the same about me. Maybe it's the adrenaline, creating that rush, or maybe it's the closest thing to emotional connection we could find, albeit a horribly unhealthy substitute for one. Whatever the reason, the point is, Rachel and I being together was less the exception and more the rule. Except for the exception of her.

Many times, those very same women said goodbye to the world before they could say hello to it. On a couple of those occasions, it had been my responsibility to make sure that

Last Pays For All

happened. And even if that didn't happen, none of them stayed with me beyond an extra day or two. I could probably recall most of their names and many of the details, maybe even have stories about good times we shared, but believe me, none of them kept me awake when I hadn't been asleep in two days, trying to figure out what my next move should be to save them.

Why was she different? Was it her? Was there something about her that reminded me of what I had given up in my life, or pointed out what I was missing now? I couldn't stop feeling the need to protect her, to take care of her, even as she demonstrated time and again that she could definitely take care of herself, and that I shouldn't always trust her allegiance to me. Maybe it was as simple as that, a core truth of people: we always want what we can't have. She had no need for me, other than the means to a paycheck end, she knew that, and when this was over, if she survived, maybe someday she'll be the one telling you a story about a good time we shared.

Was it me? Was it possible that enough time away had finally allowed my body and soul to leech out all the toxins that my life's work had filled me with? Maybe there was some truth to people being able to change in their later years. In some way, I know I'm facing my mortality in a way I never did with work. Then, death was just a risk that was part of the job. We knew it every time we punched the clock, so much so that after a while you either joke about it or dismiss it altogether. Now that I was (or at least had been) living a more normal life, I was finally coming in tune with normal experiences and emotions, one of which was not wanting to die alone. Rachel, for whatever reasons, and despite all my misgivings, had become the one I wanted to grow old with.

The Chief came down the hall, and I looked close enough to being asleep that he was satisfied. That satisfaction didn't include trust, however, and not only did he shut the door behind him, I heard him lock it from the outside. I listened even more carefully, and soon enough, I heard him pass through the front door. My own self will couldn't keep me from obsessively turning over the idea of Rachel in my mind, but outside influence, and the opportunity to act on it, was going to do the trick. I counted very slowly, backwards from one hundred. Unlike most people, who fall asleep long before they get to the end, this activity sharpened my focus and woke me up.

I had work to do.

Last Pays For All

Chapter 30

Everybody has a place where they do their best thinking. Some will tell you it's in the shower, or another certain space in the bathroom. Others have a special spot in their backyard, or maybe a favorite chair in the den. Even if you aren't aware of exactly where it is, you have one yourself. Mine was a stool at Barnacle Bob's. It might seem like a pointless thing to be doing, sitting on my ass when I'd just been running my mouth off about how I had to find Rachel, but there was a reason behind it.

Admitting the Chief was right was never an easy thing for me to do, but right now I had to. Not about Rachel; that's something I'll accept when I see her dead body, but about tracking down the mystery kidnapper. When there's water to see in every direction, and no way to keep track of who's coming and going, it makes a haystack's needle look like the size of a telephone pole.

Even if I wanted to start a search, I would have to make certain assumptions that could end up being wrong. Assumption one was that it was a privately owned boat and not one that somebody had rented. It's kind of hard, in this day and age, to convince people that the person with her wrists zip tied behind her back really wants to be going on the boat, and all the extra cleaning fees in the world might not be enough for some people to ignore the blood stains when the boat is returned. Granted, if you're some sort of diabolical person who kidnaps and kills people for money, you're probably not too concerned with returning the boat in the first place, security deposit be damned.

If I accept that it's a private boat, personally owned and operated, and not a rental nor even a charter hire, I still have no way of knowing where it left from, when it left there, where it went to or when it might be back. There is no FAA-like administration, making sure that everybody files a report about what their intentions for the day are. That's part of the live and let live attitude that makes Key West so attractive to so many people. You want to go take your boat out for the day and avoid the rest of the world? Have at it. Just don't touch the coral or catch the wrong fish. For me to find one particular boat, I'd have to go to every marina, check every slip, meet with every deckhand, and even then, where would I start?

"Yeah, hi, I'm looking for a certain boat, went out sometime this morning probably, had one guy on it, maybe more, and possibly a woman who looked less excited about the trip than anyone else. No, I'm not sure the name of the boat, or the size, or color, or the style, or anything. Can you help me find it?"

And the one person who might be able to help me, even with such limited information, was missing just as surely as Rachel was.

I didn't see Smitty as a bargaining chip, though. I liked the guy, and I would always feel bad for introducing him to the world that would get him killed, but there was no emotional bond between us. They had to know that, that ransoming his life for my knowledge would get them nowhere, so I assumed their interest in him was strictly material. They wanted him to tell them what he knew about me and my boat.

Last Pays For All

My boat! I'm a fucking exhausted idiot! The Chief was determined to keep me away from my boat, not because he wanted to keep an eye on me – if that had been the case, why leave the minute he thought I was asleep – but to keep me from getting an eye on what was going on there.

"Jersey! Hold my tab. I'll be right back." I thought about it for a second and made a better decision. The way things were going in my life, I couldn't count on any guarantees, so I slipped a couple of bills under the half-finished bottle and made for the dinghy dock.

Nothing seemed to be different from when I'd been there a few hours earlier with Scarlett, but even that opened a new kettle of fish. Maybe bringing her there had been a bad idea, especially if she was working for the kidnapper. Too bad I couldn't ask her about it now. The stuff I'd given her was designed to keep her asleep through most of the day, and probably groggy through the rest of the night. I felt bad for any customers who came looking for a high energy performance tonight from her.

I stood back up on the deck, convinced nothing was missing, but equally worried something was going to be. I'd never felt more vulnerable than I did right then, and it made me remember the feeling of standing on Scooter's deck my first visit after he'd been found. I was worried about eyes on me then, and it seemed like a good worry to have now.

Pulling my dinghy out, I made my way about fifty yards before turning right and starting a big clockwise circle. People don't often take pleasure cruises out here, especially not in an eight-foot boat with a five-horsepower engine, and whenever somebody did, it usually made the right people nervous. Anyone with something to hide would know that I was looking for something, but luckily for them, none of them interested me. I knew all my old neighbors. It was new ones I was looking for.

The third time was no more charming than the first two. If there was anything new going on out here, they were doing a damn good job of keeping it hidden. Now I was presented with a dilemma that I didn't think could work out for me, regardless of what decision I made.

As pointless as sitting at Barnacle's may have seen, at least there I would have a chance to hear talk about what was happening on the water. It was a slim hope, but a hope nonetheless, that somebody saw something strange enough that they wanted to talk about. People are still children, regardless of what their drivers' licenses say, and they like to gossip. If I stayed out here, I'd have nobody to talk to but myself, and I wasn't sure I could trust what I had to say.

The advantage to staying here was that eventually, somebody would come for me. I don't know exactly what it was anybody thought I knew, or was capable of doing, but apparently it was enough to make me the hottest property on the free agency market. I already knew two of the interested parties, and even if all they were interested in was finding the missing collection of gold and jewels that Scooter was responsible for stealing, that was reason enough for them to pay me a visit. There were several other interested parties, all of whom had their intentions hidden enough that the only thing I could do concerning them was to keep myself scarce until I had a better understanding. That, ultimately, was the reason why I couldn't just sit around here. If those people would show up first, I would no longer be the finder but the findee, and not knowing what they wanted would put me in a difficult place to negotiate with them. I had to make sure I danced with the date I brought.

Last Pays For All

That, and I couldn't stand the thought of just sitting around.

On my way back in, I passed Harper's boat and saw her where I usually did, sitting top side reading a book. I thought about heading over there, asking her if she'd seen anything funny, and wondering if she could do one more favor for me, but decided against it for that very reason.

Everybody tells stories about how they had one last mission, one more score, one last favor, and then they'd be free from whatever obligation forced them back into action in the first place. Rarely, if ever, did that one last thing work out well, and I certainly harbored no illusions that this one was going to be any more successful. I didn't want to rope her into something that could be dangerous for her, even if I knew she could handle her own in most situations and not be convinced or coerced into doing anything she didn't want to do on her own, so I passed her by, hoping I was making the right decision.

I would find out much later the decision had already been made for me.

Terry

Chapter 31

I've spent a lot of time telling you that I don't believe in coincidences, maybe more than you'd like me to, and maybe more than I should have. By the time I got back to Barnacle Bob's, my stool, along with all the rest, were taken, so I grabbed my beer and headed off to a side hustle bar, where I found myself wedged a little too uncomfortably next to some boat rats having a vicious, if harmless, argument.

"I'm telling you, bruh, it's the dumbest name for a boat, ever."

"Fuck you, man. It's a great homage."

"You want to homage a fucking ghost ship? You might as well tell your crew that someday they're all gonna mysteriously die, so they better be okay with that."

"Man, that shit ain't gonna happen. And in the meantime, think of all the free publicity you'd get. People be talking about your boat for days!"

"Talking about, yeah, but going on it? Fucking never, man."

"I don't care what you say, bruh. I think it's a great name. You're just an idiot."

"Oh, I'm the idiot? Fuck you man."

"Dude, I'm just kidding."

"No. Fuck you, Todd. Let's find out who the idiot is. Hey mister." I knew he meant me, but I was doing my best to become invisible. "Hey buddy, you." He punctuated that with a tap on my shoulder. Next time, I'll have to try harder at the invisibility. In the meantime...

"What do you want?"

"I need your help settling an argument."

"Do it like me and my friends used to. Punch each other until one of you is knocked out. The guy still standing is right."

His friend, the one named Todd, thought this was funny, but he didn't. "No man, I'm serious. This is some serious shit, and we need your opinion."

The funny thing was that I could see in his eyes that it was. Whatever the ship naming thing was all about, it meant something to him. You're not likely to find a group of people more superstitious than sailors in general, and this guy specifically was playing the part.

"Okay, then. What's the question?"

"Do you think it's a stupid idea to name a ship after the Mary Celeste?"

"You see," his friend started talking, "the Mary Celeste was this ship, and they found it once..."

"Shut up, Todd." I told him, and he did. "Everybody knows the story of the Mary Celeste. Are you saying there's a boat down here named the Mary Celeste?"

"No, but it might as well be. The Celestial Maria."

So much for Todd staying shut up. "It's not even the same thing."

"No Todd, it's not, but it's damn close enough to make a person think."

"So, you agree with me, that it's a stupid name for a boat."

"On the face of it, yeah. I mean, I'm sure the person who named the boat had a special reason for it, but until you met that person and knew what that reason was, it'd be safe to assume that it's a stupid name."

"What kind of reason could they possibly have to choose a name like that?"

I knew the exact reason they chose that name, but I wasn't going to tell them nor was I going to waste time coming up with fake answers. Instead, I changed the subject. "Where did you see this stupidly named boat?"

"Out at the Dry Tortugas."

"Has it been there a while?"

"Pulled in this afternoon, like just after noon, but then, nothing."

"Nothing?"

Todd chimed in again. "Dude, like really nothing. Once the captain weighed anchor, he went below deck, and that was it. Nobody showed their face again."

"That is odd. Go all the way out there, and then not do anything to enjoy the place. You sure nobody came on deck?"

"Dude, nobody the whole time we were out there."

"Well, you know why that is, don't you?" I asked them. They both gave me a scared, blank look, surprised that I might know something about this boat. "It's because it turned into a ghost ship. Nobody came out because there was nobody there."

Todd, bless his drunken, gullible heart, saw right through me. "But what about the captain?"

"Well, you can't have a ghost ship without a ghost. Just goes to show you that, yes, it was a stupid idea to name the boat that."

The rational one (if there had to be one, it was whoever Not-Todd was) turned to Todd with a slap across the chest. "See? I told you it was a dumb name."

116

Last Pays For All

"Well, if it was a ghost ship, we should've checked it out."

"Why didn't you?"

"We had our boss and his family with us, the kids were snorkeling all day out there, and we had to kinda keep an eye on them."

"Kinda?"

"The boss's new girlfriend was supposed to be doing that, but she and the boss, they, umm, they, well, you know."

It was kind of cute to hear how uncomfortable the thought of two people having sex made Not-Todd, but it also made me question if they'd be able to do what I needed them to. The mention of a family sounded good, though.

"Your boss, his new piece of ass and the kids, where are they now?"

"Back at the house, having dinner."

"I see." I thought subtlety and nuance would be lost on them, but it didn't stop me from playing a slow game. "And I'm guessing you guys have to take them back out for the sunset."

"No man, we're off until tomorrow."

"That's why we're having the brews, bruh." Todd held up a bottle of St. Louis's finest bottled water to make his point.

"So, why not grab a cooler full of brews, take the boat, and go find out if it's a ghost ship or not?"

Todd was all for my idea. At least, I guess that's why he started hooting and hollering, doing a duck walk with a fist pump back and forth the length of the bar. Not-Todd was less excited, but before he could say anything, I had to ask.

"Your boss lets him take care of his kids?"

"Umm, not really," he smirked a little when he spoke. "Todd mostly does the clean-up duties and hands out the water toys, but he doesn't have much responsibility."

"At least not for anything alive. That's probably a good thing." I finished my beer. "C'mon, let's go have an adventure."

I could see Not-Todd's misgivings, maybe connected to the myth of ghost ships, were actually deeply rooted in the reality that the boat was not his, he could get in a lot of trouble with his boss, especially if the Coast Guard caught us and found he had been drinking before operating the boat. Add to that the difficulty he would have finding a new job, and the fact that he was supposed to be going on a date with what was, frankly, the hottest boat captain on the wharf in a couple of hours, he had plenty of reasons to not go on an adventure, all of which I washed away with a simple response.

"Did you boys move down here to follow the rules, or to have fun?"

Last Pays For All

Chapter 32

Okay, so it took a little bit more than just the clever turn of a phrase to convince Todd and Not-Todd to take part in this little adventure. I'm not sure how much it would cost to refuel, nor what the usual pay and tip was for such a trip, but however much money I put in their hands turned out to be more than enough.

"Hey Jeannette, it's me, I'm sorry, but I'm gonna be a couple of hours late tonight. I just booked a super chill last minute charter that's hooking me up fat, like, pay my rent fat, so I had to take it. But I'll text you when we're pulling back into the harbor. 'K." He hung up the phone with one hand as he swung us around the breakwater with the other. "How quickly do you want us to get there?"

"I want to arrive right after sunset."

"Oh man, sunset out there is banging!"

"That ain't the pleasure part of this cruise, Todd." I turned back to Not-Todd. "I want enough natural light, so I can check out the boat, but not so much that everybody knows who we are. That might be good advice for you as well, so you don't get in too much trouble."

"Light doesn't matter," Not-Todd explained. "People will recognize the boat simply by the color and markings, even in twilight. The best hope we have is that the only people who'll notice will be other captains, and they'll talk to us. Hell, most of them wouldn't even be able to pick our boss out of a line-up."

Terry

"Bonus for you, then." We were pulling through the channel, just looking like one of the number of anonymous boats making its way out for the sunset. From the shore, people who were lined up at Mallory Square, or were drinking at the Sunset Pier, saw us and for a moment imagined the life we must be living, that we could be so fortunate to be out on the water. The closest they could come to it was a landlocked seat, but they wanted us to know they envied us, and were somehow proud of us, that we could live so carefree, and waved. Todd waved back to seemingly all of them, Not-Todd gave a subtle salute here and there, but I just silently watched them, wondering what it would be like to trade lives with them for a day and bury this shit in someone else's soul.

We made the turn into the Northwest Channel, and that was when Not-Todd separated us from the rest of the pleasure seekers by dropping the throttle. The roar of the engines was loud enough that hanging out back there was going to make talking a bitch, and for the time being I didn't have a whole lot to say anyway, so I made my way up front and struggled to light a cigarette in the wind. No sooner had I succeeded when Todd decided to join me.

"Can I bum one of them?"

I gave him one and a reproach. "It's going to be a long trip if you didn't bring any smokes with you, especially on the way back."

"We'll just make sure we rationalize them for the trip." He lit his effortlessly, the motions of a man repeating an act for the infinite time, and then laughed a cloud of smoke. "I mean, ration them."

I decided then it would have been worth twice my money to have taken only half the crew. "What's this 'we' shit,

Skeezix? First of all, they're my smokes, so I'll decide who smokes them when. Secondly, I never said anything about coming back with you two."

Give the kid credit. He quickly understood the severity of who I was and tried to change the subject. "She ain't going to wait for him."

"Who isn't going to wait for whom?"

"Jeanette, back at the bar. He's dopey for her, but she's got about a half dozen guys wrapped around her finger. If she is there, I bet she makes a point of leaving with someone else, just to fuck with him."

"Seems unnaturally angsty for someone who's supposedly an adult."

"Just showing him that she won't be stood up." I nodded sagely, as if we were discussing the Socratic method and not carnal relations. Todd felt like sharing something else. "You know he's wrong, right."

"Who is?"

"Him." He thumbed over his shoulder toward the bridge.

"About the girl?"

"About this boat. It can't be a ghost ship. There ain't no such thing." I fixed him with a cold, dead stare before looking out over the ocean. "Is there? You really think it's a ghost ship."

"No," I told him truthfully. "Not yet."

Terry

Chapter 33

After our brief conversation about spirituality, Todd decided he'd enjoy the cruise a lot more hanging out with Not-Todd, which was fine with me. I wish I could say it gave me time to plan, which it did, or would have, if I knew what kind of plan I should be making. I wandered back to the captain's deck just once, as much as to get a sense of how much longer we had as to make a peace offering to Todd in the form of a cigarette. Not-Todd mentioned something then; now, as we idled up on the southeast side of the islands, having made better time than he anticipated, he elaborated on what worried him about our ghost ship.

"If you are doing anything other than just passing through, you need to stop, go onto Garden Key, and get a permit. Nobody did that in the three or so hours we were there."

"Maybe they did it ahead of time."

"There is no ahead of time. The park ranger needs to meet you, and, if he so desires, check out your boat. Out here, you're on federal ground."

"Water," Todd corrected him.

"Whatever. You don't just pull up, drop anchor, and act like you own the place."

Unless, of course, you've made arrangements ahead of time to do just such a thing. And since you can't do something like that legally...

"You remember where you saw them?"

Last Pays For All

"West side of the fort, in the anchorage area."

"Okay. Here's what I need you to do. We need to do a loop, make sure that they're still out there. I need you to be sure we pass between what is left of the setting sun and them, so we look like a silhouette to them. I need you to then bring us back behind the fort, as close to it as we can get without being in their line of vision, and finally, I need you to do it all at a speed that would make anyone watching who didn't know any better just think you're a couple of guys trying to catch the sunset before heading back home, and not look like you're doing anything, you know, suspect."

"Couple of guys?" Todd decided to show off his math skills. "But there's three of us. Doesn't make that us a few?"

I crouched down, low enough below the sight line that, from a distance, my head just looked like another throw pillow on the sofa. "No, it doesn't." I tossed him a few cigarettes, to keep him occupied. "Because I ain't here."

Not-Todd was definitely the brains of the operation. He followed my commands so perfectly he didn't even acknowledge them, just looked over the charts, plotted a course, and started driving. Todd was a little more confused, possibly finally understanding just how many rules I was intending to have them break, but Not-Todd was quick on that uptake as well. "Bruh, get over here, and bring me a beer."

Doing as he was told, he tried asking a question. "Should I get him one?"

"Him, who? Just you and me. I think we'll do a nice counter-clockwise trip around the island. I always thought they gave us the best views." I readjusted myself, following his advice. I guess Todd was still watching me, because Not-

Terry

Todd felt the need to speak up again. "Bruh, just watch the sunset, and nothing else."

Other boats came and went, but there were very few anchored out for the duration. Todd was doing a perfect job not only of keeping us on a sightseer's track and tempo, but also making sure we'd be able to get convincingly close enough to the Celestial Maria without looking like we were coming up to borrow a cup of sugar. The current was running in such a way that I wouldn't be able to read the stern until we were almost by it, but the pallor of fresh abandonment that hung over the boat told me it was the one. It would look perfectly normal tied off to a dock in a marina, as if the owners had just stepped off, and the crew, only moments earlier, had finished cleaning and detailing it. But out here, with nowhere to go, it was eerily silent and empty.

It was positioned perfectly in the water for people to be on the back deck, watching the last of the sun sink into the water, wondering if the orange tendrils would make it all the way across the waves and touch the boat, but there was nothing back there for us to see except the name. This was my ghost ship.

Todd was smart enough to not floor the engine and get us out of there when we finally put the Celestial Maria behind us. Even after we were well out of its line of sight, he kept the throttle at a steady speed while I pulled myself from my cramped position and tried to rub the circulation back into my legs.

"You guys have any plastic shopping bags on board?"

"Down in the kitchen." Not-Todd looked at me, I looked at Todd, and Todd took the hint.

"When you get back, besides the other captains that

might come up to you, asking about your little unauthorized pleasure cruise, you might get some people asking who the third person was with you."

"You think someone saw you out here?"

"Not likely, but many people saw us back at the bar, whether they remember it or not." Todd was back, and I started emptying my pockets into the first bag, gun included. "If anyone asks who was with you, this is the one time in all of this it will serve you best not to lie." I tied off the first bag and dropped it into a second.

"That means, you're finally going to tell us the truth about something?"

There was a third bag, but instead of tying that one closed, I looped it through my belt first. "You tell them it was Tricky Dick you were with."

"And what do I tell them when they ask what happened to you?"

"Those unlucky enough to know who I am will be smart enough to not want to know the answer." I told them as I rolled off the side of the boat into the ocean. I looked up from the waves at them. "Count to one hundred, and then start heading for home like none of this ever happened."

For their own safety, I hoped that they did, but I couldn't worry about that now. I had my own shit to take care of.

Terry

Chapter 34

The current was working for me in more ways than one. Not only was it allowing me to take nice easy strokes so I could conserve my energy a bit, it was directing me towards the south shore of the island. It would look strange for anyone to emerge from the water after dark, especially fully clothed, but it would look far less strange if that person at least emerged from the swimming area that was adjacent to the camping area.

For better or worse, I could tell there was a good chance somebody would see me. The camping area was certainly small (small islands tend to have that problem), but it seemed plenty full of tents. I figured I'd have better odds with what I needed to do with a larger group, maybe six or eight people, than a smaller one. A couple, out on their own, would present less people for me to have to instruct, or intimidate, depending on what the situation warranted, but it also gave me less likelihood of finding someone my size. On top of that, I could meet three or four couples, all of whom would be the wrong ones for what I needed, but all of them would now know a stranger walked among them. Odds are one of them would call out the ranger before I did. I certainly needed him on the scene, but on my terms and my turf.

Sidling through the shadows hard up against the water, I found a clearing that had five tents gathered around what would eventually be a campfire. There were a couple of guitars as well, and I got a sickening feeling I might have to remember all the words to "If I Had a Hammer" before they'd agree to help me. My guess was they were out watching the sunset and would be back shortly. I could have chosen a seat now, ready to surprise them when they made it back, but that presented the same advanced notice risk the multiple couple plan had, so instead I found a dry-ish mangrove root to sit on while I emptied my sea bag and waited.

Sure enough, they were back within a few minutes, and a few minutes after that the fire was crackling, the liquor was flowing, and the guitars were strumming. I circled around, still in the shadows, so that when I entered the circle, I had them all in my line of sight.

"Evening folks. Sure looks like a festive time going on here."

They were a naturally friendly group of people, although I'm sure the marijuana I smelled in the air helped that along, and welcomed me to join them without asking any questions or really paying attention. It was when I just stood there, not moving, that any of them seemed to think twice about me. The first thing they picked up on were my wet clothes.

"Where did you swim from?"

"Key West. How long have you been camping out here?"

"Since yesterday."

"I'm guessing that means you've had a chance to meet the park ranger?"

"Yes."

"Nice guy?"

"Pretty much."

"Would you recognize him if you saw him?"

One of the guys laughed. "Kind of hard not to, with the

green uniform he'd be wearing." That guy hadn't been part of the conversation to this point, and at that point, he decided he didn't want to be part of it again and turned to the majority of the people there. There had only been two people really talking to me, one of them a serious looking woman, the other a guy who seemed serious about her. Problem was, I needed the attention from the entire class, and not just the two most studious.

"I need all the guys to stand up."

"Why?" One of the guitarists asked me this while tuning up, his focus far more on his strings than on what he was saying.

"Because I'm in a bad mood and it'll make me feel better."

Another woman pushed a joint in my direction. "This might make you feel better instead. You certainly need to chill out."

"Or at least tell us what happened to the boat you swam here from." This was the serious woman. I'm sure she was fun and liked to enjoy herself, otherwise why would she have been invited to a party on the beach, but she was also someone who had to know why things were the way they were, and I didn't feel like having that conversation.

Since nobody was standing up, I just started moving through the crowd, some with eyes on me, others pretending I wasn't there. Sure enough, there was one guy who looked to be my size, at least enough so that his clothes won't look ridiculous on me one way or the other. "Do me a favor, buddy. I need you to stand up for a second."

He gave a half snort as he decided to indulge me, even turning a slow three-sixty so I could see the whole package. "You like what you see?"

I liked it enough to know it would work for me. "I need a

change of your clothes." One of his friends, who I guess decided now was when he'd had enough, started to get lippy. Without thinking, the gun was out of my shorts, in my hand and pointed at him. "Believe it or not, I'm one of the good guys, and I'd like to keep it that way."

As always, the gun had a way of silencing the conversation, the guitars, even the bugs in the trees. Now it was my turn to look around, and I finally saw a couple of faces I recognized. Being a dick to people I don't know is a lot easier than doing it to people I do know. "I know this is what you kids call a buzzkill, and if I could tell you everything that was going on, I would. But I know some of you, and I like some of you, and even though some people might tell you otherwise, I try to keep the people I like alive. If I told you what I was doing here, that wouldn't be something I could guarantee. So, if you don't mind, some dry clothes."

My guy stepped into his tent and got me the clothes. I didn't exactly relish changing in front of them, but I couldn't risk them being out of my line of vision. Least I could do to hopefully distract everyone from my brief nakedness was to keep talking. "I need two more favors. I need one of you to find a reason to convince the ranger to join us. Without," I hastily added, "telling him that I have a gun, or that something gun related is going on. If he gets alarmed, other people will get alarmed, and that's when bad things will happen. Two, I need you, my fashion designer, to stay in your tent and play dead until I tell you otherwise."

My lippy friend didn't like me taking control. "There's ten of us. What's stopping us from rushing you and just taking you out?"

"You mean, besides one of you getting shot? The fact that

Terry

I brought a carrot to go with my stick." I took out a stack of bills. "Now, let's just play nice for the next hour or so, and we'll all be fine."

The serious woman was the one who made the call to the ranger. She told him that they're going to be playing some music, having some beers, and would he like to join? He refused, but I could tell by the tone of her voice that he was going to come and was just playing along. Sure enough, when she hung up the phone she assured me he was on his way.

"All kidding aside about his spectacular green uniform, would you recognize him as the guy you met yesterday?"

"Definitely."

"And did you spend enough time with him that you think he'll recognize all of you?"

"As in," this was serious woman's serious boyfriend, "will he know you're a stranger?"

"Exactly."

"He'll know if we tell him."

"But we won't do that, will we?" It wasn't my fault he chose the moment I was putting the gun back in my waistband to speak, but it certainly helped to prove my point. His girlfriend came to his defense. "Are you familiar with Chekov?"

"Not very, other than knowing his name and that he wrote depressing plays about depressing people in the depressing Russian countryside."

"He also said that if you introduce a gun in the first act, you need to use it by the third."

"Meaning?"

"Meaning I'm afraid you're going to have to use that gun at some point, and I don't like how it's probably going to end up."

"Believe me honey, there are a few more people who are going to like it far, far less than you are."

We sat around the campfire in a semi-awkward silence, one that could not be allowed to last.

"Look, if you invited this guy to join us for beer, music and good times, he's gonna find it a little strange when none of that is happening when he gets here."

"Strangers with guns have that kind of effect on people."

"Then don't think of me as a stranger. My name's Richard, but most people call me Tricky Dick."

One of the guitarists spoke up. "I've seen you around the Pelican a lot, though not much lately."

"Don't take that personally. Yeddie's an old friend of mine, so I used to go there for the advice more than the music. Play me a reason to change my behavior."

Thankfully, he did. Most people in the group, if they were concerned about this odd turn of events, weren't letting it bother them, and the party picked back up where it should have been all along. I guess strangers with money have that kind of effect on people as well.

A few minutes later, the ranger joined us. It took me about one second of looking at him to know he was as much a park ranger as I was a Catholic. Even though the uniform fit him fine, he wore it awkwardly, as if the first time he put it on was a few hours ago. Also, there was that whole "having a beer with the campers" thing that he proceeded to do.

"Just be sure not to mention this if you post a review on TripAdvisor, okay?" he laughed at us. He scanned the crowd, but there was no hesitation in his eyesight when he saw me. Perfect.

Terry

After a couple of minutes of everyone relaxing and enjoying themselves, I brought up the mystery boat in the anchor field. "That's one sweet looking boat. Wonder who owns something like that."

"Somebody with more money than I'll ever make on my government salary." He laughed again, trying just a little too hard to seem casual.

"Yeah, but you must know who it is. Don't they have to fill out paperwork, or get a permit or something, if they're gonna anchor out here?"

"Oh yeah, they do, but they, uh, they did it all online. Sent in their form a couple of days ago, so I haven't seen them since they arrived."

I played along. "Oh right. My friend was telling me that now. We looked into it before. He said we could submit the, um, the, what was it? The f/u 86 form?"

"That's the one," he confirmed. I turned to the serious woman.

"This ain't the ranger, is it?"

She hesitated. She didn't want to answer, because she knew that no matter what she said, it was going to get her trouble with somebody. Honestly, I didn't care what she said. I just needed the attention on her for a moment, so that after he turned to look at her, when he turned back to me, he'd be looking down the barrel of my gun.

Last Pays For All

Chapter 35

"Nice and slow, there, buddy boy. You're going to stand up and put both hands on top of your head."

"You can't pull a gun on a government official," he warned me.

"Good thing I'm not. Now, hands on your head like you're trying to keep your brains inside while you stand up slowly, just like I'm doing."

He did both of those things, the entire time gauging the distance between the two of us. Now was when he finally let the charade go. "They told me you were coming."

"They didn't bother telling you what I looked like?"

"They told me they didn't have to, and that you would come and find me."

I gotta be honest, friends and neighbors. I wasn't too comfortable with how many times they knew my next move before I did. Especially since I felt like I was just making this up as I went along.

"Well, here I am. So, what am I going to do next?"

"I know what you're not going to do. You're not going to fire that gun."

He was mostly right. The last thing I needed was a group full of witnesses filing reports with the police and the F.B.I. about a shooting. It was actually to my benefit if the shooting happened out here, this being federal property and the Chief having some connections deep in the government, but I'd already seen how his influence was slipping locally, and that meant I couldn't count on contribution from a higher level. But if I had to, I would, and he was going to try to make sure I had.

He jumped to his left, reaching for the closest hostage he could. I moved on him, aimed squarely for a spear to his chest, but my needed-to-be surgically repaired left knee, that of the recent bullet wound, didn't feel like cooperating nicely, and my attempt was more of a staggering reach. I caught him enough to spin him around, but not enough to take him out completely. Entangled, he forgot about the woman he'd been grabbing and focused on the man he'd grabbed. Each of us were trying the best we could to disable the other while also preventing them from shooting us, the result being that of a Saturday morning cartoon, two characters rolling around in a cloud of dust with the occasional arm or leg rising above the fray before being lowered back into action. This went on for about fifteen seconds, when one of the guitarists decided to change his tune.

He'd been smart enough to swing it sideways, catching the ranger with the harder wood on the curve of the body instead of the flat back, and he'd been lucky enough to not have hit me by accident. But that wasn't what he admitted to when I pushed the half-conscious ranger off of me.

"I didn't care which one of you I hit."

"Thanks, that's comforting. I'm the good guy, remember?"

To demonstrate that, I rolled the ranger onto his face, retrieved his gun, and then rolled him face up, when I smacked him in the face. "Get up, sunshine. I need you to take me to them."

He laughed. "What if I don't? You gonna kill me right

here?"

"If I don't, they will."

"These kids?"

"Your bosses. And I know you ain't going to kill me. For whatever reason, I'm too valuable to them."

He laughed again. "Damned if I know why. You're just some washed up spook who stuck his nose in where it didn't belong."

I grabbed him by the collar of his shirt and hoisted him to his feet. "I didn't stick my nose anywhere. Other people have been doing the sticking for me. Let's go." I looked back at my new friends. "I ain't going to tell you not to report this or not to tell anyone. You're going to do what you want, and I'm guessing most people won't bother believing you, especially when you got one friend who can't corroborate your story."

"Who would that be?" Always the serious person with the serious question.

"The friend in the tent. You can come out now." He did immediately.

"Holy shit, what did I miss?"

"Nothing worth talking about." I turned to the guitarist who'd done the swinging. "When's the next time you're at the Pelican?"

"This weekend."

"Buy yourself a new guitar between now and then, and bring the receipt." I turned to my doppelganger. "That's when I'll return your clothes. If they're in any condition worth returning."

I pushed the ranger into the darkness, and as soon as we left the glow of the fire, tongues were loosened, and they started talking over each other, trying to process the last fifteen minutes of their lives. I didn't bother trying to make out what they were saying. I had other things on my mind.

One way or another, I was on my way to end this.

Last Pays For All

Chapter 36

They had brought the boat in as close to the fort as they could. One spot, on the far side from the campground, had the clearance where they could nestle it up against the seawall that ran the perimeter. But that clearance didn't last long.

"They got a high tide timeline, and if you ain't with them when the tide starts to go out, we're both good as dead."

"You are, maybe."

"What makes you more valuable than any other dirtbag out there?"

"I got people from about five different countries, not to mention a very major religion, trying to kill me. Can you say the same?"

He couldn't, so he shut up, which was good with me. During the walk, he'd been ambling us straight across the vast open area in the middle of the fort when I decided that might not be a good idea. It took a bit of pistol whipping, but I finally got him to tell me where they were going to be. High ground is always the best in situations like this, so I took us into the fort and up to the ramparts. Yes, we were a little more visual this way, silhouetted by the moon as we were, but thankfully there were plenty of fortifications to hide behind. That was where we were now, looking down on the boat.

Nearby it, on a sandy spit of land, there was a dinghy beached. My guess was that was how my new best friend here had gotten ashore, but he was gracious enough to tell me I was an idiot.

"Not only didn't they tell me what you looked like, they didn't want me to know what they looked like. I got a phone call last night, offering me the job. Twenty minutes later, a courier showed up with a boat ticket and a stack of fresh hundreds, so this morning, I caught the Yankee Freedom just like any other joker."

The logic behind his words made me wonder who'd been on the dinghy. Somebody had been sent ashore, why else would it be there? That meant I had more on my plate than just storming the boat. Trying to take care of a new threat meant having to get rid of the old one. Problem was, if things went sideways tonight, and I managed to live without getting my answers, this guy might have information I could use. His lucky day, I guess.

The packed dirt softened the thud of his sleeping body as he hit the ground, a fresh pistol barrel sized wound across his temple. I didn't bring much in the way of restraints, and I couldn't afford to have him wake up early and wander around, finding a way to blow off into the ether. The shoelaces from his boots would have to do the trick.

Thankfully, they were long enough that I managed to hogtie him through the belt loops on the back of his pants. This way, if he did wake up early, he'd have a hell of a time working his way to freedom, not to mention a legendary headache. In case it took too much time for him to get free, I didn't want him roasting in the sun tomorrow morning, so I put him in a headlock and dragged him into the shadow of a cannon. He was heavier than he seemed, and deadweight is the worst weight of all, so even though the cannon was only fifty feet away, I was exhausted by the time I got there. Him safely nestled in what would be life preserving shade, I slumped against the open end of the weapon, trying to catch my breath, when I heard a familiar voice in my ear.

"Tricky? Is that you?"

Terry

Chapter 37

Whispering in my ear while hiding in a cannon is a very brave thing to do. I wouldn't have had to aim, just fire one shot and be done with it. Steel strong enough to support an explosion and a thirty-pound cannonball would have no problem ricocheting a nine-millimeter slug until it hit flesh. But the voice was just familiar enough that it kept both my guns from being drawn.

A pair of hands appeared in the diffused moonlight, and what to my wondering eye should appear but a miniature deckhand who previously disappeared.

"Smitty!" I yelled, much louder than I should have, as I helped drag him the rest of the way out. "Holy shit! How the hell did you end up here?"

"Last night, me and a couple of guys were fucking around on jet skis, tearing up and down the streets, when all of a sudden I got clotheslined. I must've bounced my head on the seat when I snapped back and knocked myself out, because when I came to, I was tied up somewhere with a hood on. Sat like that for hours, nobody saying nothing to me, nobody answering me, nothing, until finally I heard Rachel's voice. Once she showed up, things started happening. They moved us, drove us around, dumped us on a boat, and then we took off. Finally, after we'd been anchored for a while, I heard them take Rachel somewhere. I knew it was getting bad, so I finally started struggling to get free. When I did, I got up on the deck and saw them arguing.

Last Pays For All

Man, I didn't even think, I just jumped in the dinghy and tore ass to shore. But by the time this all happened, there was nobody left on the island, so I just hid, hoping to make it through the night." All those words had come rushing out of him like a torrent, but now he finally stood and took a breath. "Is this the danger you warned me about when we first met?"

I was so happy to see him and so mad at myself for putting him in this line of danger, I almost wanted to hug him. "Yeah, Smitty, this is it. But I promise you, I'm going to get you out of this. Even if it kills me."

(I know what you're thinking: How fucking dumb am I? Me, the guy who has railed against coincidences and how they don't exist, ever. Me, the guy who has torn open every story he gets told to pull apart the lies and find the truth that is trying to be hidden. Me, the guy who has learned the only way to survive is by not trusting anybody. You read that, didn't you, what he was saying, saw all of the gaping holes in it, and were yelling at me to run, shoot, do something, anything other than believe him, right? What can I say, maybe I am fucking dumb. Or just human.

Anyway...)

"Is it going to kill me?" he asked.

"Maybe," I had to answer him honestly. It felt like the right thing to do, if not the only thing. His eyes glazed over, and I could tell how scared he was. I wanted to do anything I could to take away as much fear as possible, so when he asked me to explain what was going on, I did something I swore I never would.

I told the whole story.

Terry

Chapter 38

It was a longer story than I had imagined it would be, and surprisingly more emotional than I would've expected, but I guess there is only so long you can keep things bottled up, especially when you're already keyed up emotionally to begin with. I told him everything that I could, even including how Scooter seemed to prove an exception to the rule, and when I got to the conclusion, that was what he focused on.

"There's some way that you can go back and do what you're not supposed to?"

"There never seemed to be. We tried it multiple times, starting with the Kennedy assassination, but no matter what we did, nothing changed. We had so many people there, that by the end it was like a cocktail party, but nothing was ever different."

"And you never figured out why that was?"

I shook my head. "The best we could do, the only theory we could come up with, we ended up calling it the Kennedy Contradiction. We were all back, just sitting around, wondering why we couldn't do it, really beating ourselves up, when somebody pointed out the obvious.

"'Say we go back there, and make it so he lives,' he said. 'If that happens, it changes so many things. Maybe it changes us, so we never exist, and what we do never becomes possible.' The general reaction to that was 'yeah, so?' but that's because nobody saw what this guy saw.

Last Pays For All

"'If we can never do what we do, then we can never go back to keep him from being assassinated. If you change history, you will change the present, and one of those changes in the present might preclude you from being able to change history.'

"It was so obvious, but none of us had been able to think about it that way. From that point on, we went into our missions knowing that we had a good chance at failure."

"You'd have to have a one hundred percent chance of failure," Smitty said, "based on that whole Kennedy thing."

"That's where it gets more interesting. Turns out some things happen in history the way they do because of us, and not just despite us."

Smitty started pacing. This was working him up way more than I thought it would, (personally, I figured the time travel stuff on its own would have been strange enough to just throw him for a loop) but I guess he was doing whatever he could to take his mind off of the potential of death.

"But that can't be true, either, because Scooter could do it, don't you see? He could do what nobody else could. But why and how?"

There was a cadence to his voice that at once both sounded familiar and didn't sound like Smitty at all. It dawned on me that I'd never heard Smitty this worked up before, but if that was the case, why did his voice still sound familiar?

"Maybe he was supposed to do what he did. Maybe he just found a loophole that none of us even considered and used it to his advantage. There's nothing to say the events of the *Margarita* weren't supposed to happen the way they did."

It wasn't a thought that had crossed my mind before, so I

wasn't surprised that it hadn't crossed Smitty's. What surprised me was now that it did, it obviously meant something to him.

"Maybe that's why we can't change it."

We? What the fuck was this we he was talking about?

And then it hit me.

I knew why I recognized his voice.

It had been him on the phone today, right before the bomb.

It had been him, all along.

And now it was my turn to be looking down the barrel of a gun.

"But I've been told that you can."

Last Pays For All

Chapter 39

"So, tell me how this works."

I was standing on the seawall that ran around the perimeter of the fort. Smitty stood between me and the beach, effectively breaking off my only obvious means of escape. He pulled a wad of hundred-dollar bills from his pocket, the same ones I'd paid him with not three days ago, and began throwing them at me, one at a time.

"I throw money at you like this, and ask you questions, right?"

Another bill.

"And you tell me what I need to know, or do for me what I need you to do."

Another bill.

"How could Scooter do something nobody else could?"

Another bill.

"Where did he go to do it, since nobody ever saw him come and go?"

Another bill.

"Why did he think you could do it, too?"

That was news to me, but asking Smitty about it wasn't going to help my situation any. "You might want to be careful with all this money you're wasting. I ain't really in the mood to help you, and the wind is just blowing it all away."

He cackled. "You think I'm worried about this? This piddling amount you thought you could buy me with?" He threw the remaining bills in the air, and they scattered in the wind. Strangely, I found myself thinking about all the unsuspecting tourists tomorrow, the vacation windfall they would be finding, and the unexpected attention it would continue to bring to them.

"Actually, I wasn't trying to buy you so much as to use you as bait and see who I could flush you out."

He snatched a bill that was still fluttering around his head and ripped it open. "You mean because of this." I assumed he was holding an RFID chip in his hand; as bright as the moon was, it was still pretty dark, and the chips are terribly small. "Who do you think put them in the bills to begin with?"

"Well, then, hey-hey!" I forced a fake level of conviviality out of myself. "Looks like great minds think alike."

"Maybe, but you're no great mind Tricky. You're just a dumb fuck with a latent talent you don't even understand. Thankfully, I know what to do with it. And if I don't, I know somebody who does."

"What do you mean, I'm no great mind?" I didn't care what he thought about my mind, or anything else. What I cared about was time.

Make all the fun you want about how bad guys go on page turning monologues right before they try to kill the good guy, thereby creating the opportunity for escape, but most of the time, they start their rambling because the good guy prods them. Look, if your career path is death, destruction, dismemberment and disorder, odds are that as a child, people didn't pay enough attention to you, you had abandonment issues, and you felt slighted and unloved. It's human nature, once somebody gives you a platform, to spout off about every injustice that you've experienced, real, imaginary or otherwise. I didn't think I'd get all that from Smitty, but all I wanted was time to figure out how in the hell I going to live to tell this story.

"You were going to put me out for bait, but you had no idea what you'd do to anyone who showed up."

"I had some idea."

"Yes, to kill them." When he said it, it sounded lame and pedestrian, so I let it go while he continued. "I knew that many different organizations would be interested in what was going on. They'd be tracking the chips and sending their best people when the chips finally started moving. Each of those people would have a service to offer me and my organization, whether they wanted to or not."

"Yeah, yeah, yeah, I get it. You were going to use them, and *then* kill them. Now I see why that makes you a great mind and me not so much. So, what did you do with your new crop of friends?"

"Nothing. It seems most of the people that are interested in all of this are even dumber than you. All of them ended up hiring the same person to do their dirty work."

Awwww, shit. One free agent working for multiple teams. I'd been warned about a certain person like that. I could see the boat shift from the corner of my eye. Somebody was moving on it, making their perfectly timed, dramatic entrance, and there was no doubt who I was going to be looking at.

"Hello, Rachel."

Terry

Chapter 40

"One of Rachel's clients, they have skills that even mine don't have. Turns out, they can do more with less than almost anyone else in the world."

"That's what happens when you have to try and constantly run your country under crippling international sanctions."

"Precisely. That same mechanical aptitude that keeps all those cars running, decades after they should have expired? Peanuts compared to what else they can do."

"Wait, you mean Cuba?" Wow, they really did do a good job of hiding how advanced they'd become beneath how backwards they made themselves look, but she corrected me.

"No, Tricky, you were right the first time. Mother Russia."

"It has to be Russia," Smitty cackled again. He was positively loving this, and I think some of that had to do with the fact that he was going to get to shoot me in just a couple of minutes. "It's always Russia in stories like this."

"Let me take a stab at what happens next," I said. "The consensus among the dregs of society is that I have some of the same abilities that Scooter had, so, unbeknownst to me, I've been auctioned off to the highest bidder. At the last second, right before the hammer fell, a loose alliance was made between the Communists and the Catholics. Russia says that they have a way to get that information from me

Last Pays For All

without my consent, and in turn for helping finance my capture, they'll help the Church and the Spaniards get back there in time to stop Scooter from plundering the ship. Once that's done, Russia will then go on their own world history rewrite tour. How'm I doing so far?"

Apparently too good. Smitty pulled his gun out. Guess I better wrap this up.

"Only thing I can't figure out is how you can kill me and still let me live. Unless that's what's taking up the main cabin in there. You got some machine in there ready to keep blood pumping and oxygen flowing, so whatever secrets are in here," I tapped the side of my skull, "stay intact long enough for you to harvest the information."

"Maybe you're a greater mind than I thought." He raised the gun.

"Wait! Doesn't a dying man get a last request? I want her to be the one to shoot me. After all she's put me through, I want to see if she has the heart."

Actually, I just wanted to see how much of a free agent she was. I wasn't keen on becoming a Russian guinea pig, but the fewer people poking around my brain, the more comfortable I assumed I'd feel. It was a moot point anyway.

"As poetic as it would be for the femme fatale to pull the trigger, I don't trust her to shoot you where you need to be shot, in order to turn you into a vegetable."

"Well, if I don't get that, give me this. Why? Don't your people have enough money? What's another four-hundred-million, give or take?"

Yeah, I know, it sounded stupid coming out of my mouth, too, but I honestly wanted to know what made all of the death, destruction and deception so important.

"It isn't the four-hundred-million we want. It's the one

million that we need."

"Well, Jesus Smitty, that sounds even pettier. Take me back to my boat. I'm sure I got that much lying around in various forms of currency."

"It isn't the monetary value. It's far more precious than that."

"How is that possible? Did you infuse it with Platinum? Encrust diamonds with it? Shed unicorn tears in it?"

"More valuable than that. The year before, we sent monks over with fabric from the Shroud of Turin. They put the fabric in the molten gold, and it was cast into religious artifacts that were to be spread to churches throughout Europe. They never made it back."

"Not going to lie, Smitty. That sounds like a good story, one I'm sure most of us would have heard if it were true."

"It's been seen as an embarrassment over the centuries, both the idea behind it and the fact they were lost. The story never even made it beyond the Vatican until 1985."

The same year that Mel Fisher finally found the *Atocha*. And if that could be found, so could the *Margarita*. I finished the rest of my realization out loud. "Once that happened, it was time to awaken the sleeper cells of Opus Dei, and start keeping an eye out for this stuff."

"It also meant an increase in studying the history of the wreck itself. Scholars poured over every scrap they could find. And last year, somebody came across a most startling tale, one uncorroborated by anyone else unfortunately, that spoke of a mystery man robbing the ship while at sea. From that point, it was just a matter of infiltrating the world of black market gold, following the obscure leads, until,"

"Until you stumbled down the right rabbit hole. And now you want to go back and beat Scooter to the punch."

Last Pays For All

"And you're going to help us do that."

"Here's what I don't get, though. If it's so valuable to you and your people, why tell me it's just a million dollars?"

"Because that's what ignorant people would sell it for. The total weight of the pieces was said to be around fifty pounds. Melted down and pounded out into saleable pieces, at what the market is now, the value would be...why are you laughing?"

Oh man, I couldn't help it. This was awesome. "Fifty pounds. You sure?"

"Yes. Why?"

"No, wait. And this gold. Would it matter if it were still in the shape of the icons or artifacts or whatever you had them molded into five hundred years ago, or is it just the gold you want?"

"Well, obviously, it would carry far more importance if it were still as it had been, but if not, we could always recreate the pieces. Why? Why is this funny?"

They do it in the movies for a reason. When the bad guy gets frustrated (and who wouldn't, when the person he wants dead is openly laughing at him?), they walk forward, holding the gun out even further. I guess it's supposed to be intimidating. I wouldn't know. I was too busy being doubled over, trying to catch my breath so I could tell Smitty just how not a great mind he was.

"You had the gold!"

"What?"

"You had the gold *in your hands*! And you pumped it all into Scooter."

"There was no gold. We filled him full of those stupid fishing weights he had, so we knew he'd sit where you could find him."

Terry

"That's what I'm telling you! The fishing weights weren't lead, they were gold!"

I wish I hadn't been laughing so hard, so I could see the look on Smitty's face as his world collapsed around him. "What are you telling me?"

"Scooter must've gotten wise at some point about what was going on. Word starts getting around that there are some people looking for fifty pounds of bizarre Catholic artifacts, Scooter goes back to his inventory, sees what he's sitting on, and realizes he's got the motherlode. So, he moves the rest of everything he has, and needs to get out of the business."

"But he can't," Rachel points out, "because he's got a business partner."

"And he can't risk Connelly finding out about this, because that would put him in a dangerous position. But he also can't bring himself to kill Connelly, even if there is anyone who could get away with it, it'd be him."

"So, instead he finds a way to move Connelly forward, get him out of the picture entirely."

"Almost entirely. Best he can do is, coincidentally enough, the same time he's about to turn up dead."

"But how would he know that?"

"Same way he knew how to get the gold in the first place." This thought put the brakes on the laughter. "Once he knew he could move at will, he was probably bouncing all over the place." Meaning he could still be waiting to show up in my future, or that he could have prevented his own murder if he wanted to, and why wouldn't he want to do that? "Once that's done, he falls off the radar for several years, before showing up down here, content to be anonymous."

Last Pays For All

"Until he can't be. His luck runs out when that scrap of history gets discovered, and that's when he needs to do something with this gold."

Smitty was finally tired of being left out of the conversation. Problem was, he didn't know a good way to fit in. "You mean to tell me, there are people out there using sacred gold to catch fish with?"

This made me laugh all over. "No, I think you're safe. The bag they gave me weighs about fifty pounds, so if anything, maybe there are just a few holy fishermen out there."

"What do you mean, gave to you? Why would you have the gold?"

"Well, whatever inept medical examiner you hired to be part of the operation felt like Scooter and I were friends, and that I would need some closure. Not sure how fifty pounds of fishing weights would serve as closure, but, hey, look on the bright side. We can just go back to my boat and get your gold."

Finally, Smitty was able to clear his head from all the confusion. "You're right, we can. It won't be the same as getting the original pieces, but it'll be far less complicated. Even if it means pulling them up from the ocean floor."

"Come again?"

He looked at his watch. "By now, what's left of the charred hull of your boat is sitting on the bottom of the ocean. But thankfully, flames that burn hot enough to destroy wood don't do the same thing to gold." I wanted to tell him that wasn't fair, taking a man's house from him, when I remembered that he probably wasn't planning on me living after tonight in the first place. "And if I don't need to deal with the Russians anymore, I guess I don't need to deal with you."

Terry

I'd like to think Rachel was smart enough to have never felt one hundred percent secure working with Smitty, and that she had a back-up plan for getting out of every situation, but if she did, the look on her face right now didn't instill that kind of confidence in me. He held the gun at her but kept an eye on me.

"You'd probably be just as happy to see her eliminated, wouldn't you Tricky? A woman like her, who knows so many of your secrets? It'd be better off for all of us if she were killed."

"You're right. It would be." I wasn't skipping the obvious, that what would ultimately be best for Smitty would be for all of us to die, but I wasn't going to get there until I had to. If I could play Smitty right, I'd never have to make it that far. "She certainly has double crossed me enough to earn me a lifetime of headaches."

"And you were so insistent on making her kill you, I feel I should extend the same courtesy to you."

"That would be nice." I sneered at her, and, God bless her heart, she wore a mask of fear.

"Maybe, but do you think I'd be dumb enough to put a gun in your hand?"

"Don't bother," I said. "I brought my own."

Last Pays For All

Chapter 41

Give Smitty some credit. The first thing he did up at the cannon, after revealing his true self to me, was to relieve me of my gun. He was even smart enough to think I might have taken the Ranger's gun when I'd knocked him out. Also, he was smart enough to not believe me when I told him I tossed it in the ocean, one gun being more than enough for the likes of a man like me. And finally, he was smart enough to pat me down, give me a good old once-over, to make sure I wasn't packing it somewhere.

Fortunately for me, he wasn't smart enough to check everywhere.

It wasn't the most comfortable spot I'd ever stuck a gun in my life, and I could only hope that if he saw the slightly odd gait I had as he walked me through the moonlight, he would believe me when I said I was chafing from the salt water. Most importantly, this uncomfortable hunk of metal shoved halfway up my ass would do me no sorts of good if I couldn't find a way to get it out when I needed it the most.

If I had been given a hundred chances, I never would have scripted a better interaction. Believe me, when he started talking, the laughter coming from me was real. I pictured him, holed up in that condo with the two dudes in black suits, pumping those bogus fishing weights down Scooter's throat, and the thought of all he wanted, everything that mattered in the world to him, literally passing through his hands, made me genuinely laugh uncontrollably. And people who laugh like that usually end up doubling over to catch their breath. It was still an awkward position, and I think I might have ripped something on the gun sight when I pulled it out (and I'm not talking about my boxers), but it was where I needed it when I needed it to be there.

Three quick shots later, Smitty was laying on the seawall. The first shot hit him the wrist, so he wouldn't be able to shoot. The second shot took out his knee, so he wouldn't be able to run. The third shot landed in his stomach, so he wouldn't be able to die.

"You can't let him live," Rachel told me.

"I could say the same about you."

"You could, but you won't."

"Why not? He made some pretty salient points. You being alive could cause me a host of future problems, most notably in the form of unexpected visitors."

"But you're forgetting that I'm already dead."

"That bullshit death certificate you had the Chief fill out?"

"Nothing bullshit about it. It's been filed appropriately. In fact, it's even led to the release of my will."

"Anybody left out there to take possession of your spy books and fake passports?"

She laughed. "No, actually some of those I'm going to need. Just like you need to kill him. Leave him out here to die, or take him back with us and save him, both give him the opportunity to come after you."

"And I will." His voice was pinched but not ragged. I could tell he was in a lot of pain but no danger of dying, not for several hours. He laughed. "And this time, it's personal."

"You sure you want those to be your final words?"

"They won't be. Because you don't have the balls to kill

me."

Sad thing, he was right. The last thing I needed for my own future well-being was a guy like this lurking around the shadows. And for a person like me, there are always shadows, too many of them in fact, nearby where my enemies can hide out. This guy, Smitty, whoever he was, I honestly believed was no more than a deckhand, simple minded and slacker driven. The fact that he could sneak under my radar so deeply and so smoothly bothered me. At least it should have, should have bothered me enough to not have any mercy and feel no qualms about killing him.

Maybe it was respect for that talent, game recognizing game as they say, and wanting to reward it, but this was no game, and it certainly wasn't some feel good movie with a message in the final scene before the credits rolled. This was as real as real got. I was means to an end for him, nothing more, and I needed to treat him the same way.

And yet, I couldn't.

How long I would have stood there, I'll never know. Rachel had been watching it all from a safe distance, and I was surprised she was still here. She easily could have jumped on the boat, fired up the engines, and been halfway to anywhere while I stood over Smitty, gun in my hand and indecision on my mind. Honestly, it might have taken the rising of the sun and the realization that I'd have a lot of questions to answer when people started finding us, before I could be driven to do anything. But she was there.

She slid herself behind me, pressing her chest against my back. Her left hand found my left arm, her right hand found the gun, her finger covering mine on the trigger. She rested her chin on my shoulder and breathed words into my ear.

"You can't be thinking about that, because there is no

connection between you two. He isn't anything other than a criminal, and the only justice left for him in the lawless frontier we all call home is right here. No jury will convict him, because someone will be paid off, and no judge could sentence him, because he'd be sprung from the prison. This is the world you've always lived in. You may hate it, and it may kill you, but it's yours. It's all you have. There is nothing else out there anymore. So clean this one up the best you can."

We pulled the trigger together.

Last Pays For All

Chapter 42

The tide was beginning to run out, which meant we needed to get the boat moving quickly. I took care of pulling up the anchor while she spun the dinghy back over to us from the beach. The other advantage of the out running tide was that it would take Smitty's body away from the fort and out towards the depths. I never bothered studying it, but if it were true that sharks could smell a drop of blood from a mile away, there would soon be a line outside the door of their latest buffet.

"I thought you didn't believe in coincidences."

"I don't."

We were speeding back in what I hoped was the direction of Key West. My knowledge of nautical things being what they were, I felt it best to trust her. (She had gotten me back and forth to Bimini, anyway). I don't know how well placed that trust was, but I wanted it to be, so I just accepted it.

"That's not what you told Smitty. About when it was that Scooter got Connelly to Cuba."

"Oh, that, yeah. Well, no, I don't think it was coincidence as much as he had run out of time waiting for a better option. I'm sure he would have preferred it to be after he was killed, but getting him there when he did, he probably gambled on it taking long enough for anyone to find him for it to matter."

"You really think he knew he was going to be killed."

"Yes, which naturally doesn't make any sense."

"Why not?"

"Why not just stop it from happening? All he has to do is not be there when it all goes down, and, presto! He's not dead."

It's never charming when a woman laughs at you. "Oh Tricky, you don't get it."

"What?"

"It's exactly what you said to Smitty. If changing the past affects the present so much that it becomes impossible to change the past, then it can't happen."

"Meaning all along Scooter had to get to the *Margarita* before it went down."

"I guess so." She thought about that implication. "Just imagine how much more powerful the Catholic Church might have become if he hadn't."

I couldn't think of that, because I was thinking of something else.

"What are you going to do when we get back to Key West?"

"There is no 'we' going back to Key West. I told you, I'm dead."

"Lots of people have been mistakenly declared dead before. It'll be a bit of a bureaucratic nightmare, but I'm sure we could undo it."

"For what purpose?"

"For the purpose of us." There. I said it. Why, I'm not sure, but I had to put it out there.

I could tell by how she composed herself in the moonlight that, even though she knew it might happen, she wasn't completely prepared for it. "There are a few people out there I need to explain myself to, especially concerning why I'm not turning you over to them. It would be kind of hard to come up with a viable explanation if I'm living with you."

"Then I'll come with you."

"I don't remember inviting you."

I couldn't tell if she meant the words to be as harsh as they sounded, if she wanted to cut off the conversation before it got any further, or if it was just a knee-jerk reaction of an answer, but it shut me up and shut me down all at the same time. I guess she wasn't aware of the finality of her words, because when I had nothing else to say, she started creating excuses for me.

"Besides, you have plenty to take care of back in Key West. I'm sure you and the Chief have a few final differences to air out, and whether you want them or not, there are several loose ends from all of this you need to tie up." She looked over at me. "Plus, from what I heard tonight, you need to deal with a burned-out boat."

I was looking mostly out over the water, zipping by us in the fullness of the night, but enough of my peripheral vision watched her studying me. She made some adjustments to the control, engaged the auto-pilot, and then sat down across from me.

"Tricky, please don't be mad at me. I didn't mean to hurt you."

"That's just it. I didn't think you could. I didn't think anybody could, not after all these years. But you, someone who could and would kill me or cross me just as soon as you needed to, got inside me."

"You didn't sound like that when you offered to kill me for Smitty."

"It was all I could think to say. Anything else would have been me offering my life for yours at that point."

"That's very sweet of you, but, as you can see, totally

unnecessary."

"But why? How? And don't tell me it's because I've been burying my emotions for so many years that it was inevitable they would erupt at some point, and that you just happened to be the right woman at the right time."

"You say the most flattering things."

"That's my point! Why now, you, after all these years? You must have come into my life for a reason, more of a reason than just helping me figure out who killed Scooter. You touched me in a way nobody has, that I didn't think anybody could. How?"

The laugh this time was quiet and sad, no more charming but certainly more heartfelt. "Oh Tricky. Did you really think you were the only person with a boat full of drugs at their disposal?"

Last Pays For All

Chapter 43

"I had to keep you close to me. Not necessarily physically close, although I'll never complain about that. But I needed you to be on my side, no matter what. I knew I was going to have to betray you from time to time, and I wanted to manage those betrayals as best I could, keeping them small, stringing other people along, so that things could unfold, and I could follow the clues. I knew that you would be able to see those things happen, if you had the time to think about them. So, I decided to cloud your mind a little."

"You mean this is all..."

"Nothing more than a steady dose of Love Potion Number Nine. The problem now is that it's addictive, and since I haven't been able to slip you any in a few days, you're going through some serious withdrawals."

It made sense and it didn't. It was true, and it couldn't be, all at the same time. It explained so much, but it left so much more to be explained.

"What about the trip to Bimini?"

"That was part of making sure it would work. These drugs work on anyone, meaning if I just slipped them to you and left you to your own devices, you'd end up chasing the first woman who told you it was a nice day. I had to create the entire illusion that I wanted to fall for you just like you were falling for me. Please don't be mad at me."

"How could I be? You've got my emotions under your control. Slip me another dose, and I'll feel obligated to forgive you anything."

"If it helps, this is the one betrayal I didn't think I'd ever have to make."

"Oh? Why is that?"

"Because I figured one of us would be dead before it got to this."

"You didn't see one of us making it through this alive?"

She shook her head. "Smitty was right. The protocol was, if you weren't going to come alive, I was supposed to render you vegetative and bring you back like that. If you don't believe me, have a look in the main cabin. You won't find a nicer I.C.U. anywhere."

I held out the handle of my gun, and when she didn't take it, I cocked the hammer and slid my hand on the grip. "Tell me where I need to shoot myself, so you can deliver the goods and earn your paycheck. I'm guessing it's somewhere in my brain, but a very specific somewhere. There's a lobe that can be destroyed to put me away forever while my heart and lungs go on, too stupid to stop, that also preserves the area that you think holds the secret. Is it here?" I rested the barrel on my temple. "Or, maybe here," sliding the gun to my forehead, "a frontal lobotomy, as performed by a nine-millimeter slug. Of course, I could just ruin your day altogether," I suggested as I held it up under my chin.

"I'm pretty sure that would ruin both our days," she informed me, while reaching up and taking the gun in both hands. "And I don't want that for either of us, not anymore."

"You sound like you're taking some of your own drugs"

"I wish I had. That would explain why I'm feeling the way I am." She took the gun and walked away, looking out over the stern of the boat. "When I took the job, I had no idea who you were. Nobody did. They all knew the shadow of you, the legacy of you, but nobody had ever met you long enough to know anything else about you. With just that, it was easy to imagine the worst things. Would you be as bad as Scooter? Would you be even worse? Or would you be so burned out that you'd simply refuse to take any part in it, just sail away from it all? That was part of why I took you to Bimini, so you couldn't leave on your own." She turned back to me. "Do you remember what we talked about on the sail home?"

Of course I did. I somehow remembered it all. "I wanted to just keep sailing. Put all of the new life I'd found behind me and try to start all over again."

"I couldn't let you do that. Not for the job and, by then, not for myself. For every lie I told you out there, you told me a truth, as much of one as I knew you could. And the more I got to know you, the more I realized I could never go through it all. I taught you to sail for one reason only, with the hope that the next morning, back in Key West, you'd wake up still wanting to go, and we could have gone together. It would have meant spending the rest of our lives on the run, chasing down those who wanted to chase down us before they found us, but I was ready to do it."

"What stopped you?"

"Traitor Vic. When I saw him sitting on your boat, it reminded me that there were so many larger things at play, things far more important to me, that I had to pay attention to. When I left for Miami, I fully intended to resign from the job, telling them there's was an easier way to find what we needed, by following Vic, but I couldn't do it."

"Because you didn't want to give up on ruining my life?'

"Because I didn't want you to get killed. The minute I said that you'd no longer be the best asset, there would be a price on your head so high, the line would look like a Wal-Mart on Black Friday."

"You're forgetting, I already had a price on my head."

"Chump change compared to what would have been offered. And you're also forgetting there was a price out to keep you alive. That night on the boat? They weren't shooting at you. Some of the people paying me to keep you around were also paying others to get me out of the way."

"I thought I had a complicated life."

"Not as complicated as the lives you make for those around you." She came back over to me. "The truth is what I made you feel for me is what I'm feeling for you, and the fucked up part about it all is that it's happened because I've gotten to know who you are. And if you got to know me, you'd stop feeling anything for me at all."

"Well, that, and if I stop taking the drugs."

"I can give you more if you want."

"They won't do me any good if you don't stick around."

"Are you inviting me to stay?"

"Are you telling me you're leaving?"

We both smiled, and for a moment, everything was perfect with the world. But moments don't last, and her smile faded. "I have to. For both of our sakes that have nothing to do with us. But don't worry. I'll always know how to find you when I need to." She looked over at the helm. "C'mon. We've got twenty minutes before I have to do anything with the steering, and part of that medical equipment is an amazingly comfortable bed."

We stood up, but before we went to the cabin, I dialed back on the throttle a bit.

"What are you doing?"

"Giving us thirty minutes."

Last Pays For All

Chapter 44

She disengaged the auto-pilot and slowed the boat to an idle just as the glow of Key West emerged from the horizon.

"If I knew you were stopping, I wouldn't have bothered getting dressed."

"That's not what I'm stopping for. This is where you get out."

"Here? In the middle of nowhere? Look, it's one thing to be able to swim from a passing boat to Fort Jeff, but swimming from here to Key West is a much bigger deal."

"Nobody said you have to swim." She pointed backwards to the dinghy.

"I'm not sure that's much safer. The waves out here are bigger than what hits me in the mooring field."

"I'm afraid that's the best I can do."

"Actually, you could do much better. You could drop me off at home."

"The one that caught on fire?"

"He was probably bluffing." She shot me a look. "He was maybe bluffing?"

"He wasn't bluffing. I heard him make the call. And I can't run the risk of pulling up next to a crime scene and having the Coast Guard try and check my registration."

"Seeing as how this boat isn't registered anywhere."

"At least not with any government agency they know about."

"Just another line item on a deep bureaucratic budget. Of

course, the name kind of gives that away. It's a bit on the obvious side."

"I wanted to be sure you'd be able to figure it out."

I moved to the back and started prepping the dinghy. "You're starting to sound like Smitty now, claiming I'm not the smartest person in the world."

"I just knew you had other things on your mind." She steadied it against the waves as I slid myself in. "Good luck, Tricky."

"With what?"

"Everything," she winked at me. "But especially getting over me."

"If what you say is right, in a few days, the drugs will be out of my system and I'll be right as rain."

"Yes, but I did what I could to make it a bit harder for you than just that."

"Why?"

"Because I'm a woman."

I was about to fire the engine when I finally put two pieces together. "Wait a second. You know who this boat is and is not registered with?"

"Yup."

"So that makes it your boat, and not Smitty's?"

She pushed me off the stern. "He thought he was working for me the whole time." She gave me the last wink I would see from her for a while. "I had all you boys eating out of the palm of my hand."

With that she slid back behind the wheel, pushed forward on the throttles, and left me in the moonlight. I watched until her running lights were fuzzy in the distance, wondering how much of anything she'd told me tonight was true. With nothing left on the far horizon for me, I gave my own boat the gas, and headed back in, anxious to see what fresh hell was waiting for me.

Terry

Chapter 45

He hadn't been bluffing about burning my boat. There was a sharp fragrance in the air, reminding me of campfires and childhood, tempered of course with the realization that back then, all that was burnt up were twigs and leaves. Tonight, my entire retirement fund had gone up in smoke.

It may sound like a nonsensical thing to do, but I had my boat designed to burn quickly if it ever started burning at all. The problem with a half-burnt boat would mean there would be an unburnt half that could be investigated, and whether that was being done by the United States Coast Guard or the henchmen of an anxious drug runner, it would reveal things that would cause me no end of problems. You can imagine my surprise then, when I found it to be much more intact than expected. It didn't look pretty, and certainly appeared to be less seaworthy than it was before, but instead of being gone down to the water line, it looked like it hadn't gotten farther than removing the mast and installing a rather large moonroof in the main cabin.

There was a small traffic jam at my stern, thanks to not only my dinghy being there, but also a small Coast Guard boat as well. One sailor was sitting there, mostly asleep, and when I approached he didn't seem too concerned with being any more awake. I just nodded at him as I walked across his bow and made my way to the back deck. Moonlight is no substitute for sunlight, especially not when there's a stream of hazy clouds floating by, but I could make out who was standing on my deck.

"Tennessee Jed. How'd you get stuck with this assignment?"

"I requested it, sir."

Not exactly the answer I expected, although, truthfully, I wasn't sure what to expect. "Why would you do something like that."

"Between you and me?"

"As in, don't tell your buddy who's back on the boat? I think we're good."

"I didn't think it'd be a good idea for us to search your boat until you got back. Nor did I think it would be good for anyone else to as well."

I smiled. "How would you like a cup of coffee, Tennessee?"

"Thank you, sir."

Terry

Chapter 46

Over coffee, he filled me in on everything that I needed to know at that point. He started with his name, but since I'm lousy with names, and he liked the nickname I'd given him, we stuck with that throughout the conversation. He'd been on duty when the call came in about a boat fire, and when he heard where exactly it was, he figured it was mine. Some quick mental maneuvering on his part put him in the position he wanted to be in. He was still under the thumb of the screw that had brought him out with the half-bogus search warrant, and he reminded his superior about how they'd been hamstrung on that investigation.

"Then, I told him that if we don't wait for you, and instead investigate the boat, whoever had you in their back pocket might get pissed, and we could be in a world of hurt."

His superior hadn't liked it, but he couldn't fault the logic. The most he allowed was to have the firefighters make sure there were no unattended hot spots below deck, and then when he asked for volunteers to man the boat until I got back, Jed was the first to raise his hand. As soon as everybody else cleared off, he told his partner to catch forty winks in the cabin and he'd take first watch.

"How long were you going to wait for me to get here?"

"Best I'd be able to do is hold out until sunrise. Shift change is six a.m., so not long after that, my guess is somebody would be coming out here to relieve me, whether

I wanted them to or not. At that point, you'd be on your own."

"Then I guess it's a good thing I got here when I did. Speaking of that, how did the fire get stopped so quickly?"

"Whoever called it in must have seen the first spark and not waited any longer. We were actually joking they must have been watching the boat, waiting for something to happen."

"Or they were the ones who lit the first match."

"We didn't think of that, probably because it doesn't make any sense."

It did in a roundabout way. In another world, one that didn't involve dead ex-coworkers, the Catholic Church, surfing pirates and talking manatees, a person with an axe to grind on me would want the boat saved, so my secrets could be exposed. Smitty already knew my secrets and was content to let them burn up and sink, or at least had been until he discovered the biggest secret of all. And anybody else wouldn't know the relationship I apparently had with some of the sailors, or how keen some of my neighbors were.

"I don't suppose you have the name of who called in the fire."

"I don't suppose you really want me to tell you."

"No, I guess not. Best to keep as many names as possible out of whatever report you need to write up." I made a mental note to swing by and thank her in person. "There is going to be a report, isn't there?"

"Unfortunately, there has to be one."

"What's it going to say about when you get back to base and have to tell your boss about my reappearance?"

"The truth, of course." He handed me his empty mug and stood up. "That, once you arrived, you allowed me a thorough examination of your vessel, including numerous, never before seen compartments, all of which were empty of any contraband. Furthermore, you explained to me that our previous visit served as a wake-up call for the lifestyle you'd been living, and you had turned over a new leaf."

"You think he's going to believe that?"

"He's going to have to, when two separate reports get submitted that say exactly the same thing."

"Sleeping beauty's going to back you up?"

"Sleeping beauty's going to have to," he said as he handed me the tie off line from my newest dinghy, so he could slip out. "That's the price you pay for getting to be sleeping beauty in the first place."

"You realized you're taking a chance, jeopardizing your career by handling this situation this way."

"I don't think so."

"Yeah? Why's that?"

"You seem like an interesting guy. And interesting people are handy to know when you live in such an interesting place."

"Be careful what you ask for. All I seem to be good at is getting people around me killed."

"No," he replied, as if he'd been thinking about it for a while. "You only get the people killed who need to be killed. You also do a good job of keeping the people alive you need that way."

They pulled off before I had a chance to say "Yeah? Ask Jessie and Johnny that."

I crossed the short expanse of the deck, other names running through my mind.

Traitor Vic.

Thomas Connelly.

174

Last Pays For All

Cornelius White.

Mike the Pipe.

They should all still be alive, but the only place they were now was inside my head, ghosts that would haunt the rest of my life. Knowing they were there now, it seemed pointless to try to go to sleep, so instead I went up front and sat in the pulpit.

I wasn't there long before I realized I wasn't there alone. Manatee flesh scraping on barnacles makes a very specific sound.

"I thought you were leaving me for good."

"I thought you wanted me to."

He was right. There was a point there where I was darker than I wanted to be, and the last thing I needed was someone or something trying to tell me the right thing to do.

"I resent the whole 'thing' thing. I'm an animal."

"Animal, scmanimal. You're basically a sentient being."

"Hmmmm, maybe. At least in comparison to the people you keep company with."

"Seems like I'll be keeping company with a few less of them."

"Maybe. But that's a good thing, isn't it?"

"In some cases. The more I know about Rachel, the more I don't know about her, and the less I should probably want her around, but I can't get myself to believe that."

"Give it a few days. Even if she was blowing a lot of smoke up your ass about those drugs, absence certainly does a lot more about making the heart forgetful than it does about making it fonder."

"She's left before, and it didn't make me stop thinking about her. Why should now be any different?"

"Because this time you know she isn't coming back." He

blew a small explosion of bubbles out of his nose. "And let's be truthful. You may not have forgotten her all those times, but you sure weren't always thinking about her."

That was a truth I knew but just didn't want to address. "I'm not as adjusted as I want to believe I am. Settling down, changing my stripes. Ultimately, that's not who I am."

"Ultimately hasn't been decided yet. But to get there, you probably have other issues to deal with. She's also not the only one who deceived you and is now out of your life."

"Do you know how many times I've been in that situation?"

"Yup."

"Know how many times I pulled the trigger and not thought twice?"

"All of them."

"Tonight, it should have been no different, but it was more different than anything else had been."

He floated for a moment, marshalling his thoughts. When he did start talking, I thought about suggesting he take more time to marshal, but I let him ramble.

"People retire, thinking it's going to be this great thing where they can finally relax and do nothing. They think it's going to be akin to a permanent vacation. But then it starts, and soon they are beside themselves. They realize they can't sit still, they can only read so many books, watch so much television, before they start talking about how bad it is, and how much they miss working. Other people tell them they need to get a hobby, take up a sport, join a club, start volunteering, anything, and some do, but most try and find that they can't. Instead, they sit around every morning, drinking their coffee, wondering what it is that they're doing wrong, and before long they realize they aren't alone at the breakfast table.

"There are only two kinds of people retirement works out for. The first are people who already have a future schedule filled out. They have golf games lined up, visits planned, hours scheduled at the soup kitchen, or whatever it takes. To them, retirement simply means wearing a different uniform and punching a different clock. They take right to it, unlike all those other people, because they never slow down, and they never get alone with themselves. Life is a marathon, but it isn't one where we are ultimately running to our grave. It is one we are running from. We are running against time, and when we slow down, time catches up to us. Not just in the settling in of old age and its assorted physical ailments, but emotionally. We see our lives, the way we lived them, and the choices we made and are now confronted by. And instinctively, our human nature goads us into believing we can fix the past, when all we can do is address it and accept it as it is now in our present.

"You're out here because you're haunted by ghosts of those you couldn't save, or worse, but those aren't the only ghosts haunting you. And the longer you stay still, or even slow down, the closer to home it's going to be.

"How old do you think he is now?"

"Probably about the same at as Smitty."

"And you'd never be able to shoot him?"

"Never."

"You sure about that?"

It's an irrational feeling, wanting to punch a manatee in the head, but that was the one I was having until I understood what he meant. If I knew it was my son standing in front of me, even if he had done as bad to me as Smitty did, or even worse, I don't think I could do it. Not after imagining what my absence has done to him all these years. But would I even know it was him? Or would he be what he has become, because of my actions: just another stranger, with another gun, in another town, causing another problem.

A terrible thought ran through my mind. Maybe I'd already shot him. Maybe my absence in his life was just as successful as David's presence in Jessie's life in keeping him out of the family business. "I'll never know, will I?"

"You might not. The only way you can have any chance of knowing that you didn't is if you can find him alive."

"That's easy to do."

"Easy in what way?" He dove under the boat, reemerging so he could scratch his back on the hull. "Easy for me to go online or make a few phone calls – that is, if I had your privilege of opposable thumbs – and find out the information, because my emotional connection with him isn't yours. The physical act is easy."

"It's everything that comes with it that's a bitch."

"Exactly. And, keep in mind I like you, Tricky. You're one of the good guys, albeit in a magnificently twisted way. But you're a child, like most men, and you don't want anyone to tell you you're wrong, you don't want to hear from anyone how bad you did them, and you don't want to admit to anyone that you're sorry."

"I am not." It would have been a grander statement if it didn't come out in such a whiny, petulant voice. He rolled over, flippers splayed to the side, and looked me in the eye.

"Who the fuck do you think you're talking to?"

"Sorry, I forgot."

"It's a Band-Aid. The whole way you've been living your life, it's just been a Band-Aid for what was wrong with you.

Last Pays For All

You didn't want to fix it, let it heal right, so you just slapped a Band-Aid on it and kept going. That's the same way you must think of it now. Grab one end, pull as hard as you can, and be done with it." He rolled back over and started swimming away. "Of course, I might as well go say the same thing to the coral reef. It probably listens better than you."

"I heard you. I'm just...processing it."

"Processing, my ass. You're thinking of ways to not do it. I'll see you around."

"Hold on a second!"

"What? It's late and I'm tired."

"From what, being a nautical Confucius? You said there were two types of people who could handle retirement, but you only described one. Maybe I can be part of that second group."

He laughed that particularly odd manatee laugh of his. "Not you, Tricky. Never you."

"Why not?"

"The second group of people are those who are too dumb to be self-aware. The world's full of them. And you," he emphasized with a splash of his tail that sent him off into the night, "are many things, but believe it or not, dumb isn't one of them."

It wasn't the best compliment I'd ever been paid in my life but, considering the number of times he's left me with much darker thoughts that have made sleep impossible, this time I somehow managed to feel good about myself as I went off to bed. It was comical to go through the motion of walking down the steps and through the hatch, seeing as there was almost nothing left of the ceiling. Everything below deck looked no worse for wear. A little sooty and a little wet, but still perfectly fine. I made my way through the main cabin and found my bed. The ceiling here was in no better shape, but as I lay back, I could tell myself that at least it wasn't raining.

And on the brighter side, my house may have almost burned down, but at least now I had a much better view of the moon.

Last Pays For All

Chapter 47

There was much I needed to take care of today, the biggest of which was finding the Chief, telling him the story, and then, depending on my mood, possibly killing him. I'd play it by ear. The bad news was, if I did kill him, I'd be right there in the station, so arresting me would be easy. The good news was, based on what I'd seen the last couple of days, I don't know if any cop could be bothered to do it.

First stop, though, was out in the neighborhood. It had become habit now to make a few leisurely laps around the boat, so she knew I was coming, a habit she was now determined to break me of.

"No need to be like an old hound, circling three times before you're finally ready to lay down. Just come on up and say hello."

"I'll try, but taking a person by surprise who has your kind of firepower handy is not something I think I'll ever be comfortable doing."

"Nonsense. You'll grow out of it just like you did diapers. I suppose you came over here to say thank you."

I laughed at the way she had of just cutting through the bullshit. "Maybe I did, or maybe I just wanted to tell you I was home for a while."

"A home you still have, thanks to me. Though I'm not sure how much longer you can call it a home."

"Thank you, Harper."

"Aw, hell, Tricky, I'm just messing with you. I don't need

anybody thanking me for doing the right thing. Especially since it doesn't seem to happen much anymore."

"I guess it doesn't, but I do mean it. I even brought a small token of my thanks."

She eyed the pot suspiciously. "Please don't take this the wrong way, Tricky, but you don't think of me as one of those people who needs milk, sugar and vanilla to enjoy their coffee, do you?"

"No ma'am, but it wouldn't matter if I did."

"Because a bachelor like you doesn't have any of that stuff in the first place." Absolutely nothing gets by this woman. "Come on aboard, and let's find out if your taste in coffee is any better than your taste in women."

"Hey, it can't be all bad. I'm spending time with you."

Harper eyed me coolly. "I am sure I am much too much woman for a man like you to handle, and that's if I were ever even foolish enough to give you a try."

I knew better to press my luck by making a joke, so I said nothing and poured out the coffee.

She filled me in on what I'd missed, in both the last couple of days while I'd been occupied, as well as the last several years before I found this place. She spoke with a wistful nostalgia, one I almost didn't think she was capable of, and a couple of times I caught her saying that it wasn't like it used to be, and probably wouldn't be again. Both times, she spoke quickly to cover that up, pointing out something that was an improvement over the old days, but I got the feeling that if she were younger, if she thought she might have a lot more life to live, she'd do it somewhere else.

"The world changes everywhere," I reminded her. "It doesn't matter where you live or what you do. If you want to live somewhere that doesn't change, you're going to need to find a way to live inside Disney World."

"I hear they're opening another new park, based on that Toy Story movie, so I guess even they change."

"Time marches on, and the only thing you can do is keep marching on with it."

"Is that what you really think, Tricky?"

"Believe me," I told her as I lit a new cigarette, "It's what I know. In the end, there ain't nothing you can do about time, no matter how hard you try."

Terry

Chapter 48

It was refreshing to have slept under the open air of the night, but it was also impossible to sleep nearly as late as I wanted to. After having taken up enough of Harper's time, it was still earlier than I wanted it to be for visiting the Chief. Old habits dying as hard as they do, I tied off my dinghy, making sure not to look underneath the dock, and settled into Barnacle's for a beer.

The usual crowd was there, drinking their usual drinks and having their usual conversations, but nothing was the same. The air was thick and slow, as if a storm was gathering itself together somewhere offshore and getting ready to visit us. Instinctively, I listened for the birds and wasn't surprised when I didn't hear them. I'd felt like this before, but I couldn't quite place it. And then, just like that, it was gone. It was almost as if I yawned, popped my ears, and suddenly I could hear again. It was perfectly normal, just another day in paradise, and I chalked it up to being more exhausted than I thought I was.

A guy sat down two seats over from me and helped himself to a cup of coffee. He was close enough for me to notice, especially considering how many empty bar stools there were, but not so close that I was obligated to say anything to him. He didn't feel the same way.

"Isn't it a little early to be drinking?"

"Isn't is a little early to be lecturing people?"

"Maybe. But you're not people, Tricky, are you?"

Last Pays For All

Are you fucking kidding me? I mean, really? When is this shit going to end? Hopefully now, I guessed.

"Listen, friend, I've had a long day." I spoke without looking at him. "And when I say day, I mean six weeks. I swear I could show you a calendar and convince you it's been two and a half years since I found Scooter's body and my life went sideways, because that's what it feels like. I'm sure you got some axe to grind with me, maybe because I insulted your mother, or maybe just because you're collecting a check, but whatever your reason is, I'm telling you, now is not the time to fuck with me, because I have no fucks left to give. I'll leave you here bleeding out from a slash on your leg or a shot in your head, and not care how many people come up to take a selfie with a dead guy. So, if you value anything in this world, and would like to keep living for it, I suggest you just take your coffee, your ledger, and your temperance lecture, and walk away."

I grant you, it was probably a lot harsher (and maybe a bit too confessional) than it needed to be, but I wasn't concerned about daintiness at this point. I figured it would do the trick. He didn't move, but at least he didn't talk.

For a minute.

And then he did.

"So, it is you who finds the body. Good. How do I look?"

Terry

Chapter 49

You get a job somewhere special, and somewhere in that job you find a pantheon of the people you are supposed to look up to. I'm not talking about becoming a claims adjuster or an actuarial or a press operator or a lab technician. I mean a real special job, one that cuts edges and moves society forward. A little who's who, hall of fame, so when people tell you stories about that one guy who did that one thing that one time, and now the entire world is different, you can see his face, smiling and unblemished, hanging on the wall every time you walk to the bathroom and say, "Someday, I want to be like him."

My job didn't have that, even if the things we were doing brought cutting edge to a whole new world. The people we were told about were phantoms and trolls, disappearing through space or lurking under dark bridges, and we were left to our own imaginations to create their faces. Sometimes, a picture would slip out, an errant photo from a family vacation, a serendipitous shot of someone strolling in the background, or a smudged Polaroid, smuggled out of Vietnam and included in an expose, and we would finally be able to put a face with a name.

He was older than that picture, but far younger than the guy who would drive everyone on this island to hate him. More importantly, there was something...more about him. That's the only word I can think of. People will tell you that they ran into someone they hadn't seen in a long time, and they felt like there was something missing about them. He was the opposite, and that odd, obscure observation was the first thing I said to him.

"Don't worry. It eventually goes away. Or rather, it gets eaten away. Slowly but surely, like erosion." A rueful tone came to his voice. "Eventually I'm going to be some humanoid version of the Grand Canyon."

I had a thousand reasons to hate this man, and I did for every one of them, but he was also the only person who could answer questions that had been bothering me so.

"Why?"

"I don't know. Every trip takes a little more out of me and leaves a little more of something else behind. It's done the same thing to you. You don't feel it yet, but you will."

"So, why?"

"Nothing I can do about it anymore. Once, I thought I had it figured out, and could come and go with ease, but something happened, I slipped somewhere." He stopped and laughed. "There's a cosmic banana peel out there, and it got the best of me, I guess."

"I don't get it."

"I can't control it much anymore. More often than not, I just keep slipping through the cracks. Another window slides open, and I find myself stepping through it. The only thing I have going for me, when it comes to that, is I know when each one is showing up and where it's going to take me."

"You mean?"

"Yes and no. I know my future, and therefore the future of people I come in contact with when I do. But don't go calling your bookie yet. Keep in mind, a lot of the future I run into is happening in the past."

Terry

"But I don't understand."

"Because you don't have to choose. That's the one loop hole left for me, the one option that doesn't make sense, and that flies in the face of everything we've learned. And it also makes me think that this is no accident, that they're punishing me. I flew too close to their star, and now they're spending eternity melting my wax."

Abby came by. "You ready?"

"Sure." I turned to him. "I don't suppose you want one."

"Why not? I'll see what all this early morning fuss is about." To her, "I'll have what he's having."

She got him a beer, placed it down, took a couple of steps away before stopping. When she looked back over her shoulder, I could tell she was trying to look at him without looking directly at him. He knew it too, and made sure to keep only his profile exposed. Finally, she walked away.

"She wants to know where she knows you from."

"It happens."

"What is this loop hole?"

He took a sip of his beer and looked around the bar before spotting it. "Over by the ladies' room, next to the ice machine, what do you see?"

I looked. "A missing piece of fence."

"And when you look through that missing piece of fence, what do you see?"

"Some odd sculptures, another fence, and the backside of a hotel. Why? What do you see?"

"My boat, the night they come for me."

"You mean you could?"

He nodded.

"But then you wouldn't..."

He shrugged his shoulders.

Last Pays For All

"I don't understand."

He shook his head. "It's their way of letting us know we are playing with things far beyond our understanding. Makes me think they probably think they chose the wrong place to set up shop."

"So, why do you go there eventually? If you know it's going to kill you, why not just keep slipping away?"

"I don't know. That's one thing that stays hidden. Maybe I just get tired of not going, you know? I mean, responsibilities to the timeline be damned, the whole reason I'm not walking through that fence now is because I want to live."

"Even though..."

"Even though I know it's changing me, killing me in a not-so-physical way. Or maybe, eventually, it's the only option left to me. It just becomes time." He glanced at his watch. "Speaking of time, you're running late."

"For what?"

"To see the Chief." I was going to ask how he knew that, then immediately realized the stupidity of the question. "But it doesn't matter. You're already too late."

"What?"

"You'll see. Don't be disappointed when you get there."

I got up from the stool and laid some money on the bar.

"I don't suppose you'll be here when I get back."

"I'm around for a couple of days, but not for you to talk to. You'll get distracted, like you always do, and by the time you think of it, I'll be gone. On my way to Paris, actually. 1924."

"Sounds like an exciting time to be there."

"How do you think Hemingway finds out about this place? Too bad it costs him his first two marriages."

"It does?"

"I'm there for a while, and I, um, sleep with both his wives."

He seemed oddly proud of that, and just like that, that something more that was about him became a little less, and I was reminded now of why I hated him, of the anguish he caused to other people. I no longer wanted to talk to him, to be near him, but since he brought it up, I felt the need to ask.

"How could you do that?"

"To Hemingway?"

"To Mike."

"Oh. That." The pride left his face. "Every day, a little bit more goes away. You can drive fifty miles an hour, and soon it will start to feel too slow. You go sixty, and the same thing happens, so it becomes seventy, eighty, ninety. You keep pushing, because you have to, and before you know it, you don't recognize the person you were, perfectly content to be driving fifty miles an hour."

"Why?"

"Why does the scorpion sting the frog? Because it's in their nature. Remember that Tricky, in everything you do. You can cut your hair, change your name, live in a new town, forge a different passport, but none of that will ever keep the frog safe when you're around."

That was more of a goodbye from him than I wanted, and I turned heel and left, thinking that maybe he was right, but I'd be damned before I took advice from some guy who slipped on a cosmic banana peel.

Last Pays For All

Chapter 50

I went up to the Sergeant at the reception counter and was surprised when he didn't tell me to go right in, or at least call back and tell him I was here.

"Can I help you?"

"I'm here to see the Chief," I replied, doing all I could to keep the dripping tone of obviousness out of my voice.

"The chief, or the Chief?" The second Chief came with a deeper voice and a lumbering shake of his arms, like some animatronic bear inviting me to spend too much money on shitty pizza.

"Whichever one is having office hours today."

He picked up the phone and worked his magic. "Hey chief, Richard Lockhart is here to see you."

A tinny and almost recognizable voice came through the earpiece, excited enough for me to hear. "Send him back."

"You heard the man."

"Thanks," thinking that this place was starting to feel as odd as Barnacle's had felt this morning. The office door was slightly ajar, and I did the preemptive knock with one hand while pushing the door open with the other.

Based on what you've picked up on the relationship between me and the Chief, the last thing you'd expect from him was an excited bear hug when I came into his office. What saved me from creating a massive incident was my body recognizing that this guy was shorter and stockier than the Chief. He managed to get his hug around my trunk, forcing both my arms in the air, and if I hadn't made the realization that this was the chief and not the Chief in the split second I did, there'd be a couple of busted collarbones and a whole ton of questions.

"Jesus, Chief Phillips. You scared the fuck out of me."

"I'm just excited to see you again, Tricky. Of course, I'm glad to see anyone!" His laugh was fun and pure and contagious, and I was happy to hear it.

"Man, I'm just as happy to see you as you are to see me."

"Sit down, tell me everything I missed."

He slid behind the desk while I pulled up a chair across from him. "The hell with me. Tell me what you've been up to."

"Family emergency, had to leave town immediately."

"Bull shit."

"I contracted a terrible disease, had to leave town immediately."

"Bull shit."

"I got tired of you, had to leave town immediately."

"You know I can find out."

He leaned into the desk, a conspiratorial smile on his face. "If anyone can, I know it's you, but those are the answers they told me to give you."

"What answer did they give you?"

"Between you, me, and everyone on this island? Acute appendicitis that needed to be treated immediately. And, since I hadn't taken a vacation in several years, coupled with the timely appearance of a perfect substitute, it was suggested that I take a little six-week sabbatical."

"Suggested?"

The smile faded. "The extra zeros in my bank account made the suggestion pretty easy to take." But I knew it

Last Pays For All

hadn't been that easy for him. Chief Phillips is as honest as the day is long, and something told me that there was more than just money involved when it came to getting his cooperation. No matter how clean some people are, somewhere there's a split on the family tree that can be leveraged enough for blackmail, or worse.

"Well, you didn't miss much."

"You sure about that? I seem to be missing an officer."

"I know what you're thinking, chief. This is the time in our relationship where I come clean, tell you about my past and what that has to do with our present. You come to understand who I am, and what I do, and that makes everything make sense. Shit like that may work for the Lethal Weapon movies, but it doesn't work in real life."

"Just tell me what I need to know."

"If you leave it up to me, I'm not saying another word, so you better come up with some questions."

I could tell he had some, but he wanted to make sure he asked the right ones in the right way, ways that didn't end up with me in handcuffs and him regretting his actions. All of that made his first question that much more unexpected.

"How many people did you kill?"

"Not nearly enough, but maybe more than I needed to."

"You're going to need to be clearer, on both those answers."

I shifted in my seat. "I'm not a huge fan of violating the fifth amendment. If we're going to be talking like this, shouldn't there be some sort of lawyer present, and perhaps an immunity deal on the table?"

By now, I'd forgotten he'd been smiling at all, and the bear hug felt like it happened years ago. "I'm pretty sure that prosecuting you is far outside my jurisdiction. I'm not asking questions for that. I'm asking so I can have some sort of understanding what's going on in my town. Respect that, Tricky, and respect me, and this will be a lot nicer than it's becoming."

"Fair enough, but remember, you asked." I told him the story, from the first dead body to now, with as much detail as I needed to include. I knew that a lot of what happened would never get out, if any of it did at all, so I skipped the parts that I thought would be confusing. I didn't want to get two thirds of the way through the story and suddenly, he's throwing up his hands, shouting "Wait, what?!" The part I focused on the most included the numerous people who were trying to kill me, some of whom might still be out there.

"I can't guarantee it," I said, wrapping things up, "but I know that things didn't turn out the way a lot of people hoped they would, and those people blame me, so there may still be some foxes sniffing around the hen house."

"And yet, even though you haven't killed enough, you also think you killed too much."

"Yeah."

"You want to explain that?"

"No." In the three years I'd been living down here, Chief Phillips and I had developed a working friendship. He was, like the manatee had said about me, one of the genuinely good guys, and it was not an uncommon sight for us to have a beer together now and then. He knew me well enough to like me when he needed to, and there was nothing that could be said or done about my killing Mike that would make it better or could make it worse. Maybe someday I'd let him ask me about it, but that day wasn't today.

"I guess part of this came about because you and

retirement weren't getting along so well."

"I thought we were. It came about because it was forced to happen," I explained to him. "But, all things being equal,"

"You miss the thrill of the hunt."

"I did."

"Well, maybe we can work things out that are mutually beneficial to each other."

"I'm listening."

"You have, well, I can't say scores to settle, that sounds too vigilante for a police chief to be saying. But, I understand that some of your past actions, while I was gone, may have been a bit higher above the radar than you would have liked them to be, yes?"

"That's a pretty accurate description."

"And I'm sure, that if in the future, you had to commit some similar action, you'd be sure to make sure that didn't happen again."

I wanted to tell him that sometimes it was out of my control, that people want to be killed where they want to be killed – and yes, I'm comfortable assuming they want to be killed, otherwise they wouldn't be fucking with me in the first place – and I could only do so much about that, but I could tell he was offering me some sort of bargain that I should be thankful for. "Absolutely."

"So, you'd be getting what you want."

"And in return?"

"In return, I want something you have. Your expertise."

"Are you offering to deputize me?"

"Hell, no. I like my job, and would like to keep it as long as possible. If I tried making you part of the force, we'd both be run out of here before the next sunset. Think of it more as being a special assistant to the force, consulting with us when we need you."

"That seems fine in theory. I mean, if it weren't for me, I don't think many people would be getting killed around here in the first place. But why are you doing this? You just said you want to keep your job, and even having me in this position could get a lot of people's noses out of whack."

"We'll keep it on the downlow as much as possible." He smiled again, finally. "Think of yourself as being my Batman, borderline mythology to everyone else, but the guy who finds the clues for me."

"In that case, I should start looking for an Alfred."

"Don't worry. I'm assuming you're right, that I won't have much use for you. But it's just nice to know you're in my corner when I need you."

"Fair enough."

"Now, onto other business." He pulled a manila envelope up from his desk. "This came for you first thing this morning, certified mail. I guess whoever sent it knew you'd be coming here today."

The return address was a local lawyer, which didn't excite me very much. Inside was a standard legal form, with all the various boxes checked properly and a notary stamp at the bottom, and a set of keys. I had to read it twice just to make sure it made sense. It still didn't, but sense and legality don't always have to match.

It was a will. Rachel's will, and she was leaving me everything which, if this will were to be believed, was all on her boat. Almost as if she knew my boat was going to catch on fire.

"What is it?"

"Nothing." I folded it up and slid it into my pocket with the keys. "Just letting me know I won the Irish sweepstakes."

"Really? I didn't think anybody won those things."

"Somebody has to, I guess." I stood up and he did as well, walking me to the door. "You don't know anybody who buys slightly burned boats that don't sail very well, do you?"

"I'm sure I could find an interested party, just as long as you don't have your eye set on too big a payout."

"I'd be willing to give it away if I had to."

"In that case, I could have it gone for you by the end of the week. Too soon?"

"Nah," I told him, thinking how many trips it would take to get my stuff moved. "That should be fine."

In the hallway, he had a funny way of saying goodbye. "You didn't come here looking for me, did you?"

"No, I had my heart set on seeing somebody else this morning, but don't take it personally."

"I don't think you should, either."

"Come again?"

"I don't know anything that happened when I was gone, and I already know more than I want to, but something tells me that whatever it was, it wasn't as personal as you might think."

"You're saying I got used for someone's motivations and to achieve a goal, and it wasn't done because they hated me and wanted to piss me off?"

"Why not? I'm using you for my own goals. But hey, at least I don't hate you. Beers this Thursday?"

It was such an abrupt change that all I could say was "Yeah, sure. Where should we go?"

"Like you go anywhere else. I'll find you."

'Why wouldn't you,' I thought. 'Everyone else does.'

Terry

I stepped out into the sunlight, a freer man than I'd been in a while, thinking that if she really wanted me to get her off of my mind, there were probably easier ways to do it than sleeping in her bed.

Last Pays For All

Chapter 51

Habit had me swing by her boat on a wide loop, just to make sure nobody was there waiting for me, the will just an elaborate ruse to have me show up somewhere I probably shouldn't. Everything looked as good as it could to a pair of sleep deprived eyes, so I headed back to my place. My plan was easy: figure out the one bag of stuff I would absolutely need, take that to my new boat, and sleep for a day and a half. I was below deck, deciding what fit that category, when the tackiest horn I'd ever heard caught my intention.

A thirty-eight-foot fishing boat had nestled up beside me. The captain I recognized from around town, and behind him was Yeddie, surrounded by a few women.

"Morning Tricky! Feel like having fun on the open water today?"

"I don't fish."

"Neither do we! At least not today. Just going to spend the day out at Snipes, enjoying life."

"You kids go have fun. I got some things to take care of."

"Aw c'mon Tricky. Don't be a party pooper." That was one of his entourage, who turned out to be Scarlett. Now, I was intrigued about joining them, both because I had a question to ask her and because of the bathing suit she was barely wearing.

"I'll go, but on two conditions. Condition one is I get to sleep until we get there, uninterrupted."

Yeddie laughed. "Fine, but you know that's basically a

thirty-minute nap, at best."

"You haven't heard condition two yet. Before we get there, I need us to get out to the open water, where the current runs fast and the depth goes on forever."

The captain informed me that was going to be a lot of extra fuel. I looked at Yeddie. Yeddie looked at the captain.

"Don't worry. He's good for it." He looked around. The female crew had nothing to say, so it was a silent unanimous vote. "Come on board."

"Just give me one minute." I slipped quickly into a bathing suit and a clean shirt, and, using both hands, grabbed the backpack. It made a solid thud when I dropped it on the deck.

"What's that?" one of the girl's asked me.

"My friend's ashes. That's why I need to get to the open ocean. And remember, no interrupting my sleeping."

They giggled in protest, but I was beyond caring. I stretched on the back bench and was asleep before we made full throttle.

Sometime later, Yeddie woke me to tell me we were there. Sure enough, the boat was bobbing up and down on four-foot swells and the water was the steel color of cobalt instead of the warm inviting hue of turquoise. I took the bag to the front of the boat and decided there was no reason to waste words or time.

"Goodbye, Angus." And believe me, fifty pounds of gold sinks just as fast as you think it does.

"Isn't the point to scatter the ashes?" the same girl from before asked me.

"Not this guy. He's already been scattered enough in his real life. Solidity was what he'd been missing." The fact that the answer made sense to nobody but me didn't bother her.

Last Pays For All

"If you're going to go back to sleep, you should do it up front. You could use some sun, and the breeze feels nice."

I finally regarded her and saw that she must have gotten her lack of bathing suit from the same store Scarlett shopped at. That reminded me. "Give me one minute. I need to talk to Scarlett."

"Okay." She moved back to her towel, spreading a second one next to her. Scarlett was sitting in back, having watched the entire exchange.

"I need to know. You see any of our friends in black suits lately?"

"No. Should I have?"

"Probably not, but somebody else let me think you might have, and I just wanted to know."

"Maybe they've finally gotten smart enough to blend in better. Here," she said, handing me a bottle of champagne and some strawberries. "You'll need these."

"You think so?"

"Probably not, but I know she likes them."

I went up front to introduce myself to my new friend. "My friends call me Tricky."

"Ooooh, I'm sure there's a good story behind that name."

There is, but I wasn't going to tell her. "What's your name?"

"Aleksandra."

"Nice name." I was about to ask her more, but apparently everyone else wanted to be where we were, and before I knew it, the boat was back to full speed, the wind was blowing fine spray across the bow, with all of us gathered there, the sky was an endless blue, the clouds were soft and fluffy, a small pod of dolphins found our wake and started swimming with us, and I was pouring champagne for everyone on another perfect day in the Keys.

And that was just fine with me.

Life's an adventure. You coming?

With Scooter's killer taken care of, will Tricky be able to slip back into his semi-private life? Or will the people who were sent to take care of him try to finish the job? What new work will he find thrust upon him by the chief of police? And will Rachel ever find her way back? Find out in…

Tricky Dick's Next Adventure

Fall 2019

Last Pays For All

Terry

Last Pays For All

Author's Notes & Acknowledgements

You need to give me a minute. I'm still cracking myself up. "Tricky Dick's Next Adventure." If that isn't the height of unoriginality, I don't know what is. What I do know is that, by next fall, the book will have a much catchier title. But I couldn't just leave you all hanging with nothing to look forward to.

Now, where was I? Oh, right…

People like using the phrase "Not my circus, not my monkeys." Well, this is my circus, I am the monkey, and if it weren't for a very talented group of ringmasters, I'd just be sitting here flinging poo all day instead of getting these books out.

The Abbott to my Costello, Chris Lang once again has read an early draft and had no problem telling me what stunk. Vickie Wagner and Tami Day are the two women responsible for editing the manuscript, making sure I appear a lot smarter than I am. If you come across a mistake, I guarantee you that was me making a last-minute change and saying to myself "How likely is it I'll screw up an eleven word sentence?" History has shown that to be very likely. Thanks, as always to Tamara Dower for keeping my website running, to Sharon, my tireless advocate both here and in Cuba now, Suzanne at Island Book, Emily at Books and Books, and Randy at the Eden House, all places here you can find your very own copy.

I also need to thank all of the people who supported me

by not just buying the earlier novels, but sharing the link, leaving reviews, and being genuinely excited about reading what came next. I have discovered many new people who have come on board the adventure, buying copies on recommendations from friends. Slowly this is beginning to grow, and I hope it continues to. (And if you haven't yet, please pop over to places like Amazon and Goodreads and leave a review. Those mean more to help spreading the word than you think.) I can honestly say you've inspired me, and even though Scooter's killer has been found, I promise you Tricky's adventures will continue.

Finally, just one word: Fiction. All of it, although I actually did a little research about Fort Jefferson and the Dry Tortugas when it came to writing that part. (Sadly, that research did not include getting back out there for a visit. Someday, I will.) And most of you who read these and have visited or live here do a good job of figuring out which part is a stand-in for what real place. If you do that, let me just say that I enjoyed my time at Gas Monkey, I really liked the people I worked with, and me blowing it up is just a coincidence.

Jack
August 30, 2018
Key West

28396305R00117